W9-ACJ-351

130959

ALSO BY AGATHA CHRISTIE:

BLACK COFFEE

A HERCULE POIROT NOVEL

by
Agatha Christie

Adapted as a novel by
Charles Osborne

Doubleday Direct Large Print Edition

ST. MARTIN'S PRESS ❧ NEW YORK

This Large Print Edition, prepared especially for Doubleday Direct, Inc., contains the complete unabridged text of the original Publisher's Edition.

ISBN: 0-7394-0002-9

**This Large Print Book carries the
Seal of Approval of N.A.V.H.**

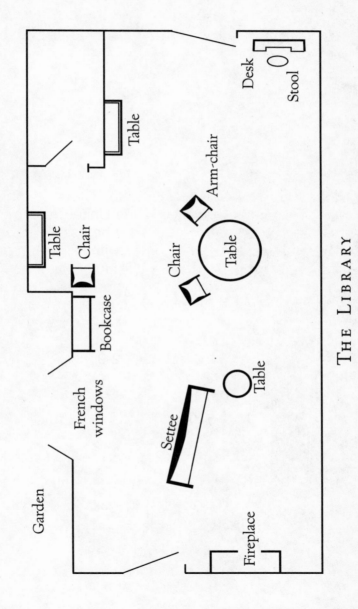

THE LIBRARY

BLACK COFFEE

CHAPTER ONE

Hercule Poirot sat at breakfast in his small but agreeably cosy flat in Whitehall Mansions. He had enjoyed his brioche and his cup of hot chocolate. Unusually, for he was a creature of habit and rarely varied his breakfast routine, he had asked his valet, George, to make him a second cup of chocolate. While he was awaiting it, he glanced again at the morning's post which lay on his breakfast table.

Meticulously tidy as always, he had placed the discarded envelopes in one neat pile. They had been opened very carefully, with the paper-knife in the form of a miniature sword which his old friend Hastings had given him for a birthday many years ago. A second pile contained those communications he found of no interest—circulars, mostly—which in a moment he would ask George to dispose of. The third pile consisted of those letters which would require an answer of some kind, or at least an acknowledgement. These would be dealt with after breakfast, and in any case not before ten o'clock. Poirot thought it not quite professional to begin a routine working day before ten. When he was on a case—ah, well, of course that was different. He remembered that once he and Hastings had set out well before dawn in order to—

But, no, Poirot did not want his thoughts to dwell on the past. The happy past. Their last case, involving an international crime organization known as The Big Four, had been brought to a satisfactory conclusion, and Hastings had returned to the Argentine, his wife and his ranch. Though his old friend was temporarily back in London on business connected with the ranch, it was highly unlikely that Poirot and he would find themselves working together again to solve a crime. Was that why Hercule Poirot was feeling restless on this fine spring morning in May 1934? Ostensibly retired, he had been lured out of that retirement more than once when an especially interesting problem had been presented to him. He had enjoyed being on the scent again, with Hastings by his side to act as a kind of sounding board for his ideas and theories. But nothing of professional interest had presented itself to Poirot for several months. Were there no imaginative crimes and criminals any more? Was it all violence and brutality, the kind of sordid murder or robbery which was beneath his, Poirot's, dignity to investigate?

His thoughts were interrupted by the arrival, silently at his elbow, of George with that second and welcome cup of chocolate. Welcome not only because Poirot would enjoy the rich, sweet taste, but also because it would enable him to postpone, for a few more minutes, the realization that the day, a fine sunny morning, stretched before him with nothing more exciting in prospect than a constitutional in the park and a walk through Mayfair to his favourite restaurant in Soho, where he would lunch alone on—what, now?—perhaps a little pâté to begin, and then the sole *bonne femme,* followed by—

He became aware that George, having placed the chocolate on the table, was addressing him. The impeccable and imperturbable George, an intensely English, rather wooden-faced individual, had been with Poirot for some time now, and was all that he wished in the way of a valet. Completely incurious, and extraordinarily reluctant to express a personal opinion on any subject, George was a mine of information about the English aristocracy, and as fanatically neat as the great detective himself. Poirot had more than once said to him, "You press admirably the trousers, George, but the imagination, you possess it not." Imagination, however, Hercule Poirot possessed in abundance. The ability to press a pair of trousers properly was, in his opinion, a rare accomplishment. Yes, he was indeed fortunate in having George to look after him.

"—and so I took the liberty, sir, of promising that you would return the call this morning," George was saying.

"I do beg your pardon, my dear George," replied Poirot. "My attention was wandering. Someone has telephoned, you say?"

"Yes, sir. It was last night, sir, while you were out at the theatre with Mrs. Oliver. I had retired to bed before you arrived home, and thought it unnecessary to leave a message for you at that late hour."

"Who was it who called?"

"The gentleman said he was Sir Claud Amory, sir. He left his telephone number, which would appear to be somewhere in Surrey. The matter, he said, was a somewhat delicate one, and when you rang you were not to give your name to anyone else, but were to insist on speaking to Sir Claud himself."

"Thank you, George. Leave the telephone number on my desk," said Poirot. "I shall ring Sir Claud after I have perused this morning's *Times*. It is still a trifle early in the morning for telephoning, even on somewhat delicate matters."

George bowed and departed, while Poirot slowly finished his cup of chocolate and then repaired to the balcony with that morning's newspaper.

A few minutes later *The Times* had been laid aside. The international news was, as usual, depressing. That terrible Hitler had turned the German courts into branches of the Nazi party, the Fascists had seized power in Bulgaria and, worst of all, in Poirot's own country, Belgium, forty-two miners were feared dead after an explosion at a mine near Mons. The home news was little better. Despite the misgivings of officials, women competitors at Wimbledon were to be allowed to wear shorts this summer. Nor was there much comfort in the obituaries, for people Poirot's age and younger seemed intent on dying.

His newspaper abandoned, Poirot lay back in his comfortable wicker chair, his feet on a small stool. Sir Claud Amory, he thought to himself. The name struck a chord, surely? He had heard it somewhere. Yes, this Sir Claud was well-known in some sphere or other. But what was it? Was he a politician? A barrister? A retired civil servant? Sir Claud Amory. Amory.

The balcony faced the morning sun, and Poirot found it warm enough to bask in for a moment or two. Soon it would become too warm for him, for he was no sun-worshipper. "When the sun drives me inside," he mused, "then I will exert myself and consult the *Who's Who*. If this Sir Claud is a person of some distinction, he will surely be included in that so admirable volume. If he is not—?" The little detective gave an expressive shrug of his shoulders. An inveterate snob, he was already predisposed in Sir Claud's favour by virtue of his title. If he were to be found in *Who's Who,* a volume in which the details of Poirot's own career could also be discovered, then perhaps this Sir Claud was someone with a valid claim on his, Hercule Poirot's, time and attention.

A quickening of curiosity and a sudden cool breeze combined to send Poirot indoors. Entering his library, he went to a shelf of reference books and took down the thick red volume whose title, *Who's Who,* was embossed in gold on its spine. Turning the pages, he came to the entry he sought, and read aloud.

AMORY, Sir Claud (Herbert); Kt. 1927; *b.* 24 Nov. 1878. *m.* 1907, Helen Graham (*d.* 1929); one *s.* Educ: Weymouth Gram. Sch.: King's Coll.: London. Research Physicist GEC Laboratories, 1905; RAE Farnborough (Radio Dept.), 1916; Air Min. Research Establishment, Swanage, 1921; demonstrated a new Principle for accelerating particles: the travelling wave linear accelerator, 1924. Awarded Monroe Medal of Physical Soc. *Publications:* papers in learned journals. *Address:* Abbot's Cleve, nr. Market Cleve, Surrey. *T:* Market Cleve 304. *Club:* Athenaeum.

"Ah, yes," Poirot mused. "The famous scientist." He remembered a conversation he had had some months previously with a member of His Majesty's government, after Poirot had retrieved some missing documents whose contents could have proved embarrassing. They had talked of security, and the politician had admitted that security measures in general were not sufficiently stringent. "For instance," he had said, "what Sir Claud Amory is working on now is of such fantastic importance in any future war—but he refuses to work under laboratory conditions where he and his invention can be properly guarded. Insists on working alone at his house in the country. No security at all. Frightening."

I wonder, Poirot thought to himself as he replaced *Who's Who* on the bookshelf, I wonder—can Sir Claud want to engage Hercule Poirot to be a tired old watchdog? The inventions of war, the secret weapons, they are not for me. If Sir Claud—

The telephone in the next room rang, and Poirot could hear George answering it. A moment later, the valet appeared. "It's Sir Claud Amory again, sir," he said.

Poirot went to the phone. " 'Allo. It is Hercule Poirot who speaks," he announced into the mouthpiece.

"Poirot? We've not met, though we have acquaintances in common. My name is Amory, Claud Amory—"

"I have heard of you, of course, Sir Claud," Poirot responded.

"Look here, Poirot. I've got a devilishly tricky problem on my hands. Or rather, I might have. I can't be certain. I've been working on a formula to bombard the atom—I won't go into details, but the Ministry of Defence regards it as of the utmost importance. My work is now complete, and I've produced a formula from which a new and deadly explosive can be made. I have reason to suspect that a member of my household is attempting to steal the formula. I can't say any more now, but I should be greatly obliged if you would come down to Abbot's Cleve for the weekend, as my house-guest. I want you to take the formula back with you to London, and hand it over to a certain person at the Ministry. There are good reasons why a Ministry courier can't do the job. I need someone who is ostensibly an unobtrusive, unscientific member of the public but who is also astute enough—"

Sir Claud talked on. Hercule Poirot, glancing across at the reflection in the mirror of his bald, egg-shaped head and his elaborately waxed moustache, told himself that he had never before, in a long career, been considered unobtrusive, nor did he so consider himself. But a weekend in the country and a chance to meet the distinguished scientist could be agreeable, plus, no doubt, the suitably expressed thanks of a grateful government—and merely for carrying in his pocket from Surrey to Whitehall an obscure, if deadly, scientific formula.

"I shall be delighted to oblige you, my dear Sir Claud," he interrupted. "I shall arrange to arrive on Saturday afternoon, if that is convenient to you, and return to London, with whatever you wish me to take with me, on Monday morning. I look forward greatly to making your acquaintance."

Curious, he thought, as he replaced the receiver. Foreign agents might well be interested in Sir Claud's formula, but could it really be the case that someone in the scientist's own household—? Ah well, doubtless more would be revealed during the course of the weekend.

"George," he called, "please take my heavy tweed suit and my dinner jacket and trousers to the cleaner's. I must have them back by Friday, as I am going to the Country for the Weekend." He made it sound like the Steppes of Central Asia and for a lifetime.

Then, turning to the phone, he dialled a number and waited for a few moments before speaking. "My dear Hastings," he began, "would you not like to have a few days away from your business concerns in London? Surrey is very pleasant at this time of the year . . ."

CHAPTER TWO

Sir Claud Amory's house, Abbot's Cleve, stood just on the outskirts of the small town—or rather, overgrown village—of Market Cleve, about twenty-five miles south-east of London. The house itself, a large but architecturally nondescript Victorian mansion, was set amid an attractive few acres of gently undulating countryside, here and there heavily wooded. The gravel drive, from the gatehouse up to the front door of Abbot's Cleve, twisted its way through trees and dense shrubbery. A terrace ran along the back of the house, with a lawn sloping down to a somewhat neglected formal garden.

On the Friday evening two days after his telephone conversation with Hercule Poirot, Sir Claud sat in his study, a small but comfortably furnished room on the ground floor of the house, on the east side. Outside, the light was beginning to fade. Sir Claud's butler, Tredwell, a tall, lugubrious-looking individual with an impeccably correct manner, had sounded the gong for dinner two or three minutes earlier, and no doubt the family was now assembling in the dining-room on the other side of the hall.

Sir Claud drummed on the desk with his fingers, his habit when forcing himself to a quick decision. A man of medium height and build in his fifties, with greying hair brushed straight back from a high forehead and eyes of a piercingly cold blue, he now wore an expression in which anxiety was mixed with puzzlement.

There was a discreet knock on the study door, and Tredwell appeared in the doorway. "Excuse me, Sir Claud. I wondered if perhaps you had not heard the gong—"

"Yes, yes, Tredwell, that's all right.

Would you tell them I shall be in very shortly? Say I'm caught on the phone. In fact, I am about to make a quick phone call. You may as well begin serving."

Tredwell withdrew silently, and Sir Claud, taking a deep breath, pulled the telephone towards himself. Extracting a small address-book from a drawer of his desk, he consulted it briefly and then picked up the receiver. He listened for a moment and then spoke.

"This is Market Cleve three-oh-four. I want you to get me a London number." He gave the number, then sat back, waiting. The fingers of his right hand began to drum nervously on the desk.

Several minutes later, Sir Claud Amory joined the dinner-party, taking his place at the head of the table, around which the six others were already seated. On Sir Claud's right sat his niece, Barbara Amory, with Richard, her cousin and the only son of Sir Claud, next to her. On Richard Amory's right was a house-guest, Dr. Carelli, an Italian. Continuing round, at the opposite end of the table to Sir Claud, sat Caroline Amory, his sister. A middle-aged spinster, she had run Sir Claud's house for him ever since his wife died some years earlier. Edward Raynor, Sir Claud's secretary, sat on Miss Amory's right, with Lucia, Richard Amory's wife, between him and the head of the household.

Dinner, on this occasion, was not at all festive. Caroline Amory made several attempts at small-talk with Dr. Carelli, who answered her politely enough without offering much in the way of conversation himself. When she turned to address a remark to Edward Raynor, that normally polite and socially suave young man gave a nervous start, mumbled an apology and looked embarrassed. Sir Claud was as taciturn as he normally was at meal-times, or perhaps even more so. Richard Amory cast an occasional anxious glance across the table at his wife, Lucia. Barbara Amory alone seemed in good spirits, and made spasmodic light conversation with her Aunt Caroline.

It was while Tredwell was serving the dessert course that Sir Claud suddenly addressed the butler, speaking loudly enough for all at the dinner-table to hear his words.

"Tredwell," he said, "would you ring Jackson's garage in Market Cleve, and ask them to send a car and driver to the station to meet the eight-fifty from London? A gentleman who is visiting us after dinner will be coming by that train."

"Very well, Sir Claud," replied Tredwell as he left. He was barely out of the room when Lucia, with a murmured apology, got up abruptly from the table and hurried out, almost colliding with the butler as he was about to close the door behind him.

Crossing the hall, she hurried along the corridor and proceeded to the large room at the back of the house. The library—as it was generally called—served normally as a drawing-room as well. It was a comfortable room rather than an elegant one. French windows opened from it onto the terrace, and another door led to Sir Claud's study. On the mantelpiece, above a large open fireplace, stood an old-fashioned clock and some ornaments, as well as a vase of spills for use in lighting the fire.

The library furniture consisted of a tall bookcase with a tin box on the top of it, a desk with a telephone on it, a stool, a small table with gramophone and records, a set-tee, a coffee-table, an occasional table with book-ends and books on it, two up-right chairs, an arm-chair and another ta-ble on which stood a plant in a brass pot. The furniture in general was old-fashioned, but not sufficiently old or distinguished to be admired as antique.

Lucia, a beautiful young woman of twenty-five, had luxuriant dark hair which flowed to her shoulders, and brown eyes which could flash excitingly but were now smouldering with a suppressed emotion not easy to define. She hesitated in the middle of the room, then crossed to the French windows and, parting the curtains slightly, looked out at the night. Uttering a barely audible sigh, she pressed her brow to the cool glass of the window and stood lost in thought.

Miss Amory's voice could be heard out-side in the hall, calling, "Lucia—Lucia—where are you?" A moment later, Miss Amory, a somewhat fussy elderly lady a few years older than her brother, entered the room. Going across to Lucia, she took the younger woman by the arm and pro-pelled her towards the settee.

"There, my dear. You sit down here," she said, pointing to a corner of the settee. "You'll be all right in a minute or two."

As she sat, Lucia gave a wan smile of gratitude to Caroline Amory. "Yes, of course," she agreed. "It's passing already, in fact." Though she spoke English impeccably, perhaps too impeccably, an occasional inflection betrayed that English was not her native tongue.

"I just felt faint, that's all," she continued. "How ridiculous of me. I've never done such a thing before. I can't imagine why it should have happened. Please go back, Aunt Caroline. I shall be quite all right here." She took a handkerchief from her handbag, as Caroline Amory looked on solicitously. Dabbing at her eyes with it, she then returned the handkerchief to her bag, and smiled again. "I shall be quite all right," she repeated. "Really, I shall."

Miss Amory looked unconvinced. "You've really not looked well, dear, all the evening, you know," she remarked, anxiously studying Lucia.

"Haven't I?"

"No, indeed," replied Miss Amory. She sat on the settee, close to Lucia. "Perhaps you've caught a little chill, dear," she twittered anxiously. "Our English summers can be rather treacherous, you know. Not at all like the hot sun in Italy, which is what you're more used to. So delightful, Italy, I always think."

"Italy," murmured Lucia with a faraway look in her eyes, as she placed her handbag beside her on the settee. "Italy—"

"I know, my child. You must miss your own country sadly. It must seem such a dreadful contrast—the weather for one thing, and the different customs. And we must seem such a cold lot. Now, Italians—"

"No, never. I never miss Italy," cried Lucia, with a vehemence that surprised Miss Amory. "Never."

"Oh, come now, child, there's no disgrace in feeling a little homesick for—"

"Never!" Lucia repeated. "I hate Italy. I always hated it. It is like heaven for me to be here in England with all you kind people. Absolute heaven!"

"It's really very sweet of you to say that, my dear," said Caroline Amory, "though I'm sure you're only being polite. It's true we've all tried to make you feel happy and at home here, but it would be only natural for you to yearn for Italy sometimes. And then, not having any mother—"

"Please—*please*—" Lucia interrupted her, "do not speak of my mother."

"No, of course not, dear, if you'd rather I didn't. I didn't mean to upset you. Shall I get you some smelling-salts? I've got some in my room."

"No, thank you," Lucia replied. "Really, I'm perfectly all right now."

"It's no trouble at all, you know," Caroline Amory persisted. "I've got some very nice smelling-salts, a lovely pink colour, and in the most charming little bottle. And very pungent. Sal ammoniac, you know. Or is it spirits of salts? I can never remember. But anyway, it's not the one you clean the bath with."

Lucia smiled gently, but made no reply. Miss Amory had risen, and apparently could not decide whether to go in search of smelling-salts or not. She moved indecisively to the back of the settee and rearranged the cushions. "Yes, I think it must be a sudden chill," she continued. "You were looking the absolute picture of health this morning. Perhaps it was the excitement of seeing this Italian friend of yours, Dr. Carelli? He turned up so suddenly and unexpectedly, didn't he? It must have given you quite a shock."

Lucia's husband, Richard, had entered the library while Caroline Amory was speaking. Miss Amory did not notice him, for she could not understand why her words appeared to have upset Lucia, who leaned back, closed her eyes and shivered. "Oh, my dear, what is it?" asked Miss Amory. "Are you coming over faint again?"

Richard Amory closed the door and approached the two women. A conventionally handsome young Englishman of about thirty, with sandy hair, he was of medium height, with a somewhat thick-set, muscular figure. "Do go and finish your dinner, Aunt Caroline," he said to Miss Amory. "Lucia will be all right with me. I'll look after her."

Miss Amory still appeared irresolute. "Oh, it's you, Richard. Well, perhaps I'd better go back," she said, taking a reluctant step or two in the direction of the door leading to the hall. "You know how your father does hate a disturbance of any kind.

And particularly with a guest here. It's not as though it was someone who was a close friend of the family."

She turned back to Lucia. "I was just saying, dear, wasn't I, what a very strange thing it was that Dr. Carelli should turn up in the way he did, with no idea that you were living in this part of the world. You simply ran into him in the village, and invited him here. It must have been a great surprise for you, my dear, mustn't it?"

"It was," replied Lucia.

"The world really is such a very small place, I've always said so," Miss Amory continued. "Your friend is a very good-looking man, Lucia."

"Do you think so?"

"Foreign-looking, of course," Miss Amory conceded, "but distinctly handsome. And he speaks English very well."

"Yes, I suppose he does."

Miss Amory seemed disinclined to let the topic go. "Did you really have no idea," she asked, "that he was in this part of the world?"

"None whatsoever," replied Lucia emphatically.

Richard Amory had been watching his

wife intently. Now he spoke again. "What a delightful surprise it must have been for you, Lucia," he said.

His wife looked up at him quickly, but made no reply. Miss Amory beamed. "Yes, indeed," she continued. "Did you know him well in Italy, my dear? Was he a great friend of yours? I suppose he must have been."

There was a sudden bitterness in Lucia's voice. "He was never a friend," she said.

"Oh, I see. Merely an acquaintance. But he accepted your generous invitation to stay. I often think foreigners are inclined to be a little pushing. Oh, I don't mean you, of course, dear—" Miss Amory had the grace to pause and blush. "I mean, well, you're half English in any case." She looked archly at her nephew, and continued, "In fact, she's quite English now, isn't she, Richard?"

Richard Amory did not respond to his aunt's archness, but moved towards the door and opened it, as though in invitation to Miss Amory to return to the others.

"Well," said that lady as she moved reluctantly to the door, "if you're sure I can't do anything more—"

"No, no." Richard's tone was as abrupt as his words as he held the door open for her. With an uncertain gesture and a last nervous smile at Lucia, Miss Amory left.

Emitting a sigh of relief, Richard shut the door after her and came back to his wife. "Natter, natter, natter," he complained. "I thought she'd never go."

"She was only trying to be kind, Richard."

"Oh, I dare say she was. But she tries a damn sight too hard."

"I think she's fond of me," murmured Lucia.

"What? Oh, of course." Richard Amory's tone was abstracted. He stood observing his wife closely. For a few moments there was a constrained silence. Then, moving nearer to her, Richard looked down at Lucia. "You're sure there's nothing I can get you?"

Lucia looked up at him, forcing a smile. "Nothing, really, thank you, Richard. Do go back to the dining-room. I really am perfectly all right now."

"No," replied her husband. "I'll stay with you."

"But I'd rather be alone."

There was a pause. Then Richard spoke again, as he moved behind the settee. "Cushions all right? Would you like another one under your head?"

"I am quite comfortable as I am," Lucia protested. "It would be nice to have some air, though. Could you open the window?"

Richard moved to the French windows and fumbled with the catch. "Damn!" he exclaimed. "The old boy's locked it with one of those patent catches of his. You can't open it without the key."

Lucia shrugged her shoulders. "Oh, well," she murmured, "it really doesn't matter."

Richard came back from the French windows and sat in one of the chairs by the table. He leaned forward, resting his elbows on his thighs. "Wonderful fellow, the old man. Always inventing something or other."

"Yes," replied Lucia. "He must have made a lot of money out of his inventions."

"Pots of it," said Richard gloomily. "But it isn't the money that appeals to him.

They're all the same, these scientists. Always on the track of something utterly impracticable that can be of no earthly interest to anyone other than themselves. Bombarding the atom, for heaven's sake!"

"But all the same, he is a great man, your father."

"I suppose he's one of the leading scientists of the day," said Richard grudgingly. "But he can't see any point of view except his own." He spoke with increasing irritation. "He's treated me damned badly."

"I know," Lucia agreed. "He keeps you here, chained to this house, almost as though you were a prisoner. Why did he make you give up the army and come to live here?"

"I suppose," said Richard, "that he thought I could help him in his work. But he ought to have known that I should be of no earthly use to him in that way. I simply haven't got the brains for it." He moved his chair a little closer to Lucia and leaned forward again. "My God, Lucia, it makes me feel pretty desperate, sometimes. There he is, rolling in money, and he spends every penny on those damned experiments of his. You'd think he'd let me have something of what will be mine someday, in any case, and allow me to get free of this place."

Lucia sat upright. "Money!" she exclaimed bitterly. "Everything comes round to that. Money!"

"I'm like a fly caught in a spider's web," Richard continued. "Helpless. Absolutely helpless."

Lucia looked at him with an imploring eagerness. "Oh, Richard," she exclaimed. "So am I."

Her husband looked at her with alarm. He was about to speak when Lucia continued, "So am I. Helpless. And I want to get out." She rose suddenly and moved towards him, speaking excitedly. "Richard, for God's sake, before it's too late, take me away!"

"Away?" Richard's voice was empty and despairing. "Away where?"

"Anywhere," replied Lucia with growing excitement. "Anywhere in the world! But away from this house. That's the important thing, away from this house! I am afraid, Richard, I tell you I'm afraid. There are shadows—" she looked over her shoulder as though she could see them—"shadows everywhere."

Richard remained seated. "How can we go away without money?" he asked. He looked up at Lucia and continued, bitterly, "A man's not much good to a woman without money, is he, Lucia? Is he?"

She backed away from him. "Why do you say that?" she asked. "What do you mean?"

Richard continued to look at her in silence, his face tense yet curiously expressionless.

"What's the matter with you tonight, Richard?" Lucia asked him. "You're different, somehow—"

Richard rose from his chair. "Am I?"

"Yes—what is it?"

"Well—" Richard began, and then stopped. "Nothing. It's nothing."

He started to turn away from her, but Lucia pulled him back and placed her hands on his shoulders. "Richard, my dear—" she began. He took her hands from his shoulders. "Richard," she said again.

Putting his hands behind his back, Richard looked down at her. "Do you think I'm a complete fool?" he asked. "Do you think I didn't see this *old friend* of yours slip a note into your hand tonight?"

"Do you mean you thought that—"

He interrupted her fiercely. "Why did you come out from dinner? You weren't feeling faint. That was all a pretence. You wanted to be alone to read your precious note. You couldn't wait. You were nearly mad with impatience because you couldn't get rid of us. First Aunt Caroline, then me." His eyes were cold with hurt and anger as he looked at her.

"Richard," said Lucia, "you're mad. Oh, it's absurd. You can't think I care for Carelli! Can you? Can you, really? My dear, Richard, my dear—it's *you*. It's nobody but you. You must know that."

Richard kept his eyes fixed on her. "What is in that note?" he asked quietly.

"Nothing—nothing at all."

"Then show it to me."

"I—I can't," said Lucia. "I've destroyed it."

A frigid smile appeared and disappeared on Richard's face. "No, you haven't," he said. "Show it to me."

Lucia was silent for a moment. She

looked at him imploringly. Then, "Richard," she asked, "can't you trust me?"

"I could take it from you by force," he muttered through clenched teeth, as he advanced a step towards her. "I've half a mind—"

Lucia backed away with a faint cry, her eyes still on Richard's face as though willing him to believe her. Suddenly he turned away. "No," he said, as though to himself. "I suppose there are some things one can't do." He turned back to face his wife. "But, by God, I'll have it out with Carelli."

Lucia caught his arm with a cry of alarm. "No, Richard, you mustn't. You mustn't. Don't do that, I beg you. Don't do that."

"You're afraid for your lover, are you?" sneered Richard.

"He's not my lover," Lucia retorted fiercely.

Richard took her by the shoulders. "Perhaps he isn't—yet," he said. "Perhaps he—"

Hearing voices outside in the hall, he stopped speaking. Making an effort to control himself, he moved to the fireplace, took out a cigarette-case and lighter, and lit a cigarette. As the door from the hall opened and the voices grew louder, Lucia moved to the chair Richard had recently vacated, and sat. Her face was white, her hands clasped together in tension.

Miss Amory entered, accompanied by her niece Barbara, an extremely modern young woman of twenty-one. Swinging her handbag, Barbara crossed the room towards her. "Hello, Lucia, are you all right now?" she asked.

CHAPTER THREE

Lucia forced a smile as Barbara Amory approached her. "Yes, thank you, darling," she replied. "I'm perfectly all right. Really."

Barbara looked down at the beautiful black-haired wife of her cousin. "Not broken any glad tidings to Richard, have you?" she asked. "Is that what it's all about?"

"Glad tidings? What glad tidings? I don't know what you mean," protested Lucia.

Barbara clasped her arms together and made a rocking motion as though cradling a baby. Lucia's reaction to this pantomime was a sad smile and a shake of the head.

Miss Amory, however, collapsed in horror onto a chair. "Really, Barbara!" she admonished.

"Well," said Barbara, "accidents will happen, you know."

Her aunt shook her head vigorously. "I cannot think what young girls are coming to, nowadays," she announced to no one in particular. "In my young days we did not speak flippantly of motherhood, and I would never have allowed—" She broke off at the sound of the door opening, and looked around in time to see Richard leave the room. "You've embarrassed Richard," she continued, addressing Barbara, "and I can't say I'm at all surprised."

"Well, Aunt Caroline," Barbara replied, "you are a Victorian, you know, born when the old Queen still had a good twenty years of life ahead of her. You're thoroughly representative of *your* generation, and I dare say I am of mine."

"I'm in no doubt as to which I prefer—" her aunt began, only to be interrupted by Barbara, who chuckled and said, "I think the Victorians were too marvellous. Fancy telling children that babies were found under gooseberry bushes! I think it's sweet."

She fumbled in her handbag, found a cigarette and a lighter, and lit the cigarette. She was about to begin speaking again when Miss Amory silenced her with a gesture. "Oh, do stop being silly, Barbara. I'm really very worried about this poor child here, and I wish you wouldn't make fun of me."

Lucia suddenly broke down and began to weep. Trying to wipe the tears from her eyes, she said between sobs, "You are all so good to me. No one was ever kind to me until I came here, until I married Richard. It's been wonderful to be here with you. I can't help it, I—"

"There, there," murmured Miss Amory, rising and going to Lucia. She patted her on the shoulder. "There, there, my dear. I know what you mean—living abroad all your life—most unsuitable for a young girl. Not a proper kind of upbringing at all, and of course the continentals have some very peculiar ideas about education. There, there."

Lucia stood up and looked about her uncertainly. She allowed Miss Amory to lead her to the settee, and sat at one end while Miss Amory patted cushions around her and then sat next to her. "Of course you're upset, my dear. But you must try to forget about Italy. Although, of course, the dear Italian lakes are quite delightful in the spring, I always think. Very suitable for holidays, but one wouldn't want to live there, naturally. Now, now, don't cry, my dear."

"I think she needs a good stiff drink," suggested Barbara," sitting on the coffee-table and peering critically but not unsympathetically into Lucia's face. "This is an awful house, Aunt Caroline. It's years behind the times. You never see the ghost of a cocktail in it. Nothing but sherry or whisky before dinner, and brandy afterwards. Richard can't make a decent Manhattan, and just try asking Edward Raynor for a Whisky Sour. Now what would *really* pull Lucia around in no time would be a Satan's Whisker."

Miss Amory turned a shocked countenance upon her niece. "What," she inquired in horrified tones, "might a Satan's Whisker be?"

"It's quite simple to make, if you have the ingredients," replied Barbara. "It's merely equal parts of brandy and crème de menthe, but you mustn't forget a shake of red pepper. That's most important. It's absolutely super, and guaranteed to put some pep into you."

"Barbara, you know I disapprove of these alcoholic stimulants," Miss Amory exclaimed with a shudder. "My dear father always said—"

"I don't know what he *said*," replied Barbara, "but absolutely everyone in the family knows that dear old Great-Uncle Algernon had the reputation of being a three-bottle man."

At first Miss Amory looked as if she might explode, but then the slight twitch of a smile appeared on her lips, and all she said was, "Gentlemen are different."

Barbara was having none of this. "They're not in the least different," she said. "Or at any rate I can't imagine why they should be allowed to be different. They simply got away with it in those days." She produced from her handbag a small mirror, a powder-puff and lipstick. "Well, how do we look?" she asked herself. "Oh, my God!" And she began vigorously to apply lipstick.

"Really, Barbara," said her aunt, "I do wish you wouldn't put quite so much of that red stuff on your lips. It's such a very bright colour."

"I hope so," replied Barbara, still completing her make-up. "After all, it cost seven and sixpence."

"Seven shillings and sixpence! What a disgraceful waste of money, just for—for—"

"For 'Kissproof,' Aunt Caroline."

"I beg your pardon?"

"The lipstick. It's called 'Kissproof.'"

Her aunt sniffed disapprovingly. "I know, of course," she said, "that one's lips are inclined to chap if one has been out in a high wind, and that a little grease is advisable. Lanoline, for instance. I always use—"

Barbara interrupted her. "My dear Aunt Caroline, take it from me, a girl simply can't have too much lipstick on. After all, she never knows how much of it she's going to lose in the taxi coming home." As she spoke, she replaced the mirror, powder-puff and lipstick in her handbag.

Miss Amory looked puzzled. "What do you mean, 'in the taxi coming home?'" she asked. "I don't understand."

Barbara rose and, moving behind the

settee, leaned over to Lucia. "Never mind. Lucia understands, don't you, my love?" she asked, giving Lucia's chin a little tickle.

Lucia Amory looked around blankly. "I'm so sorry," she said to Barbara, "I haven't been listening. What did you say?"

Focusing her attention on Lucia again, Caroline Amory returned to the subject of that young lady's health. "You know, my dear," she said, "I really am worried about you." She looked from Lucia to Barbara. "She ought to have something, Barbara. What have we got now? Sal volatile, of course, that would be the very thing. Unfortunately, that careless Ellen broke my bottle this morning when she was dusting in my room."

Pursing her lips, Barbara considered for a moment. "I know," she exclaimed. "The hospital stores!"

"Hospital stores? What do you mean? What hospital stores?" Miss Amory asked.

Barbara came and sat in a chair close to her aunt. "You remember," she reminded her. "All of Edna's things."

Miss Amory's face brightened. "Ah, yes, of course!" Turning to Lucia, she said, "I wish you had met Edna, my elder niece,

Barbara's sister. She went to India with her husband—oh, it must have been about three months before you came here with Richard. Such a capable girl, Edna was."

"Most capable," Barbara confirmed. "She's just had twins. As there are no gooseberry bushes in India, I think she must have found them under a double mango tree."

Miss Amory allowed herself a smile. "Hush, Barbara," she said. Then, turning back to Lucia, she continued, "As I was saying, dear, Edna trained as a dispenser during the war. She worked at our hospital here. We turned the Town Hall into a hospital, you know, during the war. And then for some years after the war, until she was married, Edna continued to work in the dispensary at the County Hospital. She was very knowledgeable about drugs and pills and that sort of thing. I dare say she still is. That knowledge must be invaluable to her in India. But what was I saying? Oh, yes—when she left. Now what did we do with all those bottles of hers?"

"I remember perfectly well," said Barbara. "A lot of old things of Edna's from the dispensary were bundled into a box.

They were supposed to be sorted out and sent to hospitals, but everyone forgot, or at least no one did anything about it. They were put away in the attic, and they only came to light again when Edna was packing to go to India. They're up there"—she gestured towards the bookcase—"and they still haven't been looked through and sorted out."

She rose and, taking her chair across to the bookcase, stood on it and, reaching up, lifted the black tin box down from the top.

Ignoring Lucia's murmured "Please don't bother, darling, I really don't need anything," Barbara carried the box over to the table in the centre of the room and put it down.

"Well," she said, "at least we might as well have a look at the things now that I've got them down." She opened the box. "Oh dear, it's a motley collection," she said, taking out various bottles as she spoke. "Iodine, Friar's Balsam, something called Tinct.Card.Co, Castor oil." She grimaced. "Ah, now we're coming to the hot stuff," she exclaimed, as she took out of the box some small brown glass tubes. "Atropine, morphine, strychnine," she read from the labels. "Be careful, Aunt Caroline. If you arouse my furious temper, I'll poison your coffee with strychnine, and you'll die in the most awful agony." Barbara made a mock-menacing gesture at her aunt, who waved her away with a snort.

"Well, there's nothing here we could possibly try out on Lucia as a tonic, that's for certain," she laughed, as she began to pack the bottles and phials back into the tin box. She was holding a tube of morphine aloft in her right hand as the door to the hall opened and Tredwell ushered in Edward Raynor, Dr. Carelli and Sir Claud Amory. Sir Claud's secretary, Edward Raynor, entered first, an unremarkable-looking young man in his late twenties. He moved across to Barbara and stood looking at the box. "Hello, Mr. Raynor. Interested in poisons?" she asked him as she continued to pack up the bottles.

Dr. Carelli, too, approached the table. A very dark, swarthy individual of about forty, Carelli wore perfectly fitting evening clothes. His manner was suave, and when he spoke, it was with the slightest Italian accent. "What have we here, my dear Miss Amory?" he queried.

Sir Claud paused at the door to speak to Tredwell. "You understand my instructions?" he asked, and was satisfied by the reply: "Perfectly, Sir Claud." Tredwell left the room, and Sir Claud moved across to his guest.

"I hope you will excuse me, Dr. Carelli," he said, "if I go straight to my study? I have several important letters which must go off tonight. Raynor, will you come with me?" The secretary joined his employer, and they went into Sir Claud's study by the connecting door. As the door closed behind them, Barbara suddenly dropped the tube she had been holding.

CHAPTER FOUR

Dr. Carelli stepped forward quickly, and picked up the tube Barbara had dropped. Glancing at it before handing it back to her with a polite bow, he exclaimed, "Hello, what's this? Morphine!" He picked up another one from the table. "And Strychnine! May I ask, my dear young lady, where you got hold of these lethal little tubes?" He began to examine the contents of the tin box.

Barbara looked at the suave Italian with distaste. "The spoils of war," she replied shortly, with a tight little smile.

Rising anxiously, Caroline Amory approached Dr. Carelli. "They're not really poison, are they, Doctor? I mean, they couldn't harm anyone, could they?" she asked. "That box has been in the house for years. Surely it's harmless, isn't it?"

"I should say," replied Carelli drily, "that, with the little lot you have here, you could kill, roughly, twelve strong men. I don't know what *you* regard as harmful."

"Oh, good gracious," Miss Amory gasped with horror as she moved back to her chair and sat heavily.

"Here, for instance," continued Carelli, addressing the assembled company. He picked up a tube and read slowly from the label. " 'Strychnine hydrochloride; one sixteenth of a grain.' Seven or eight of these little tablets, and you would die a very unpleasant death indeed. An extremely painful way out of the world." He picked up another tube. " 'Atropine sulphate.' Now, atropine poisoning is sometimes very hard to tell from ptomaine poisoning. It is also a very painful death."

Replacing the two tubes he had handled, he picked up another. "Now here—" he continued, speaking now very slowly and deliberately, "here we have hyoscine hydrobromide, one hundredth of a grain. That doesn't sound very potent, does it? Yet I assure you, you would only have to swallow half of the little white tablets in this tube, and"—he made a graphic gesture. "There would be no pain—no pain at all. Just a swift and completely dreamless sleep, but a sleep from which there would be no awakening." He moved towards Lucia and held out the tube to her, as though inviting her to examine it. There was a smile on his face, but not in his eyes.

Lucia stared at the tube as though she were fascinated by it. Stretching out a hand, she spoke in a voice that sounded almost as though it were hypnotized. "A swift and completely dreamless sleep—" she murmured, reaching for the tube.

Instead of giving it to her, Dr. Carelli glanced at Caroline Amory with an almost questioning look. That lady shuddered and looked distressed, but said nothing. With a shrug of the shoulders, Carelli turned away from Lucia, still holding the tube of hyoscine hydrobromide.

The door to the hallway opened, and Richard Amory entered. Without speaking he strolled across to the stool by the desk and sat down. He was followed into the room by Tredwell, who carried a tray containing a jug of coffee and cups and saucers. Placing the tray on the coffee-table, Tredwell left the room as Lucia moved to sit on the settee and pour out the coffee.

Barbara went across to Lucia, took two cups of coffee from the tray, and then moved over to Richard to give him one of them, keeping the other for herself. Dr. Carelli, meanwhile, was busy replacing the tubes in the tin box on the centre table.

"You know," said Miss Amory to Carelli, "you make my flesh creep, Doctor, with your talk of swift, dreamless sleep and unpleasant deaths. I suppose that, being Italian as you are, you know a lot about poisons?"

"My dear lady," laughed Carelli, "is that not an extremely unjust—what do you say—*non sequitur*? Why should an Italian know any more about poisons than an Englishman? I have heard it said," he continued playfully, "that poison is a woman's weapon, rather than a man's. Perhaps I should ask you—? Ah, but perhaps, dear lady, it is an Italian woman you were thinking of? Perhaps you were about to mention a certain Borgia. Is that it, eh?" He took a cup of coffee from Lucia at the coffee-table and handed it to Miss Amory, returning to take another cup for himself.

"Lucrezia Borgia—that dreadful creature! Yes, I suppose that's what I was thinking of," admitted Miss Amory. "I used to have nightmares about her when I was a child, you know. I imagined her as very pale, but tall, and with jet-black hair just like our own dear Lucia."

Dr. Carelli approached Miss Amory with the sugar-bowl. She shook her head in refusal, and he took the bowl back to the coffee tray. Richard Amory put his coffee down, took a magazine from the desk and began to browse through it, as his aunt developed her Borgia theme. "Yes, dreadful nightmares I used to have," Miss Amory was saying. "I would be the only child in a room full of adults, all of them drinking out of very elaborate goblets. Then this glamorous woman—now I come to think of it, she did look remarkably like you, Lucia dear—would approach me and force a goblet upon me. I could tell by the way she smiled, somehow, that I ought not to drink, but I knew I wasn't going to be able to refuse. Somehow, she hypnotized me into drinking, and then I would begin to feel a dreadful burning sensation in my throat, and I would find myself fighting for breath. And then, of course, I woke up."

Dr. Carelli had moved close to Lucia. Standing in front of her, he gave an ironic bow. "My dear Lucrezia Borgia," he implored, "have mercy on us all."

Lucia did not react to Carelli's joke. She appeared not to have heard him. There was a pause. Smiling to himself, Dr. Carelli turned away from Lucia, drank his coffee and placed his cup on the centre table. Finishing her coffee rapidly, Barbara seemed to realize that a change of mood was called for. "What about a little tune?" she suggested, moving across to the gramophone. "Now, what shall we have? There's a marvellous record here that I bought up in town the other day." She began to sing, accompanying her words with a jazzy little dance. " 'Ikey—oh, crikey—what *have* you got on?' Or what else is there?"

"Oh, Barbara dear, not that vulgar song," implored Miss Amory, moving across to her and helping to look through the gramophone records. "There are some much nicer records here. If we must have popular music, there are some lovely songs by John McCormack here somewhere. Or what about 'The Holy City'?—I can't remember the soprano's name. Or why not that nice Melba record? Oh—ah, yes—here's Handel's *Largo*."

"Oh, come on, Aunt Caroline. We're not likely to be cheered up by Handel's *Largo*," Barbara protested. "There's some Italian opera here, if we must have classical music. Come on, Dr. Carelli, this ought to be your province. Come and help us choose."

Carelli joined Barbara and Miss Amory around the gramophone, and all three of them began to sort through the pile of records. Richard now seemed engrossed in his magazine.

Lucia rose, moved slowly and apparently aimlessly across to the centre table and glanced at the tin box. Then, taking care to establish that the others were not observing her, she took a tube from the box and read the label. " 'Hyoscine hydrobromide.' " Opening the tube, Lucia poured nearly all of the tablets into the palm of her hand. As she did so, the door to Sir Claud's study opened, and Sir Claud's secretary, Edward Raynor, appeared in the doorway. Unknown to Lucia, Raynor watched her as she put the tube back into the tin box before moving over to the coffee-table.

At that moment Sir Claud's voice was heard to call from the study. His words were indistinct, but Raynor, turning to answer him, said, "Yes, of course, Sir Claud. I'll bring you your coffee now."

The secretary was about to enter the library when Sir Claud's voice arrested him. "And what about that letter to Marshall's?"

"It went off by the afternoon post, Sir Claud," replied the secretary.

"But Raynor, I told you—oh, come back here, man," Sir Claud boomed from his study.

"I'm sorry, sir," Raynor was heard to say as he retreated from the doorway to rejoin Sir Claud Amory in his study. Lucia, who had turned to watch him at the sound of his voice, seemed not to realize that the secretary had been observing her movements. Turning, so that her back was to Richard, she dropped the tablets she had been holding into one of the coffee-cups on the coffee-table, and moved to the centre of the settee.

The gramophone suddenly burst into life with a quick foxtrot. Richard Amory put down the magazine he had been reading, finished his coffee quickly, placed the cup on the centre table, and moved across to his wife. "I'll take you at your word. I've decided. We'll go away together."

Lucia looked up at him in surprise. "Richard," she said faintly, "do you really mean it? We can get away from here? But I thought you said—what about?—where will the money come from?"

"There are always ways of acquiring money," said Richard grimly.

There was alarm in Lucia's voice as she asked, "What do you mean?"

"I mean," said her husband, "that when a man cares about a woman as I care about you, he'll do anything. Anything!"

"It does not flatter me to hear you say that," Lucia responded. "It only tells me that you still do not trust me—that you think you must buy my love with—"

She broke off and looked around as the door to the study opened and Edward

Raynor returned. Raynor walked over to the coffee-table and picked up a cup of coffee, as Lucia changed her position on the settee, moving down to one end of it. Richard had wandered moodily across to the fireplace and was staring into the unlit grate.

Barbara, beginning a tentative foxtrot alone, looked at her cousin Richard as though considering whether to invite him to dance. But, apparently put off by his stony countenance, she turned to Raynor. "Care to dance, Mr. Raynor?" she asked.

"I'd love to, Miss Amory," the secretary replied. "Just a moment, while I take Sir Claud his coffee."

Lucia suddenly rose from the settee. "Mr. Raynor," she said hurriedly, "that isn't Sir Claud's coffee. You've taken the wrong cup."

"Have I?" said Raynor. "I'm so sorry."

Lucia picked up another cup from the coffee-table and held it out to Raynor. They exchanged cups. "That," said Lucia, as she handed the cup to Raynor, "is Sir Claud's coffee." She smiled enigmatically to herself, placed the cup Raynor had given her on the coffee-table and returned to the settee.

Turning his back to Lucia, the secretary took some tablets from his pocket and dropped them into the cup he was holding. As he was walking with it towards the study door, Barbara intercepted him. "Do come and dance with me, Mr. Raynor," she pleaded, with one of her most engaging smiles. "I'd force Dr. Carelli to, except that I can tell he's simply dying to dance with Lucia."

As Raynor hovered indecisively, Richard Amory approached. "You may as well give in to her, Raynor," he advised. "Everyone does, eventually. Here, give the coffee to me. I'll take it to my father."

Reluctantly Raynor allowed the coffee-cup to be taken from him. Turning away, Richard paused momentarily and then went through into Sir Claud's study. Barbara and Edward Raynor, having first turned over the gramophone record on the machine, were now slowly waltzing in each other's arms. Dr. Carelli watched them for a moment or two with an indulgent smile, before approaching Lucia who, wearing a look of utter dejection, was still seated on the settee.

Carelli addressed her. "It was most kind of Miss Amory to allow me to join you for the weekend," he said.

Lucia looked up at him. For a few seconds she did not speak, but then said, finally, "She is the kindest of people."

"And this is such a charming house," continued Carelli, moving behind the settee. "You must show me over it sometime. I am extremely interested in the domestic architecture of this period."

While he was speaking, Richard Amory had returned from the study. Ignoring his wife and Carelli, he went across to the box of drugs on the centre table, and began to tidy its contents.

"Miss Amory can tell you much more about this house than I can," Lucia told Dr. Carelli. "I know very little of these things."

Looking around first, to confirm that Richard Amory was busying himself with the drugs, that Edward Raynor and Barbara Amory were still waltzing at the far end of the room, and that Caroline Amory appeared to be dozing, Carelli moved to the front of the settee and sat next to Lucia. In low, urgent tones, he muttered, "Have you done what I asked?"

Her voice even lower, almost a whisper, Lucia said desperately, "Have you no pity?"

"Have you done what I told you to?" Carelli asked more insistently.

"I—I—" Lucia began, but then, faltering, rose, turned abruptly and walked swiftly to the door which led into the hall. Turning the handle, she discovered that the door would not open.

"There's something wrong with this door," she exclaimed, turning to face the others. "I can't get it open."

"What's that?" called Barbara, still waltzing with Raynor.

"I can't get this door open," Lucia repeated.

Barbara and Raynor stopped dancing and went across to Lucia at the door. Richard Amory moved to the gramophone to switch it off before joining them. They took it in turns to attempt to get the door open, but without success, observed by Miss Amory, who was awake but still seated, and by Dr. Carelli, who stood by the bookcase.

Unnoticed by any of the company, Sir Claud emerged from his study, coffee-cup in hand, and stood for a moment or two observing the group clustered around the door to the hall.

"What an extraordinary thing," Raynor exclaimed, abandoning his attempt to open the door, and turning to face the others. "It seems to have got stuck somehow."

Sir Claud's voice rang across the room, startling them all. "Oh, no, it's not stuck. It's locked. Locked from the outside."

His sister rose and approached Sir Claud. She was about to speak, but he forestalled her. "It was locked by my orders, Caroline," he told her.

With all eyes upon him, Sir Claud walked across to the coffee-table, took a lump of sugar from the bowl, and dropped it into his cup. "I have something to say to you all," he announced to the assembled company. "Richard, would you be so kind as to ring for Tredwell?"

His son looked as though he were about to make some reply. However, after a pause he went to the fireplace and pressed a bell in the wall nearby.

"I suggest that you all sit down," Sir Claud continued, with a gesture towards the chairs.

Dr. Carelli, with raised eyebrows, crossed the room to sit on the stool. Edward Raynor and Lucia Amory found chairs for themselves, while Richard Amory chose to stand in front of the fireplace, looking puzzled. Caroline Amory and her niece Barbara occupied the settee.

When all were comfortably seated, Sir Claud moved the arm-chair to a position where he could most easily observe all the others. He sat.

The door on the left opened, and Tredwell entered.

"You rang, Sir Claud?"

"Yes, Tredwell. Did you call the number I gave you?"

"Yes, sir."

"Was the answer satisfactory?"

"Perfectly satisfactory, sir."

"And a car has gone to the station?"

"Yes, sir. A car has been ordered to meet the train."

"Very well, Tredwell," said Sir Claud. "You may lock up now."

"Yes, sir," replied Tredwell, as he withdrew.

After the butler had closed the door behind him, the sound of a key turning in the lock could be heard.

"Claud," Miss Amory exclaimed, "what on earth does Tredwell think—?"

"Tredwell is acting on my instructions, Caroline," Sir Claud interrupted sharply.

Richard Amory addressed his father. "May we ask the meaning of all this?" he inquired coldly.

"I am about to explain," replied Sir Claud. "Please listen to me calmly, all of you. To begin with, as you now realize, those two doors"—he gestured towards the two doors on the hall side of the library—"are locked on the outside. From my study next door, there is no way out except through this room. The French windows in this room are locked." Swivelling around in his seat to Carelli, he explained, as though in parenthesis, "Locked, in fact, by a patent device of my own, which my family knows of, but which they do not know how to immobilize." Again addressing everyone, Sir Claud continued, "This place is a rat-trap." He looked at his watch. "It is now ten minutes to nine. At a few minutes past nine, the rat-catcher will arrive."

"The *rat-catcher?*" Richard Amory's face was a study in perplexity. "What rat-catcher?"

"A detective," explained the famous scientist drily as he sipped his coffee.

CHAPTER FIVE

Consternation greeted Sir Claud's announcement. Lucia uttered a low cry, and her husband stared at her intently. Miss Amory gave a shriek, Barbara exclaimed "Crikey!" and Edward Raynor contributed an ineffectual "Oh, I say, Sir Claud!" Only Dr. Carelli seemed unaffected.

Sir Claud settled in his arm-chair, holding his coffee-cup in his right hand and the saucer in his left. "I seem to have made my little effect," he observed with satisfaction. Finishing his coffee, he set the cup and saucer down on the table with a grimace. "The coffee is unusually bitter this evening," he complained.

His sister's countenance registered a certain annoyance at the aspersion cast on the coffee, which she took as a direct criticism of her housekeeping. She was about to say something, when Richard Amory spoke. "What detective?" he asked his father.

"His name is Hercule Poirot," replied Sir Claud. "He is a Belgian."

"But why?" Richard persisted. "Why did you send for him?"

"A leading question," said his father, with an unpleasantly grim smile. "Now we come to the point. For some time past, as most of you know, I have been engaged in atomic research. I have made a discovery of a new explosive. Its force is such that everything hitherto attempted in that line will be mere child's play beside it. Most of this you know already—"

Carelli got to his feet quickly. "I did not know," he exclaimed eagerly. "I am much interested to hear of this."

"Indeed, Dr. Carelli?" Sir Claud invested the conventionally meaningless phrase with a curious significance, and Carelli, in some embarrassment, resumed his seat.

"As I was saying," Sir Claud continued, "the force of Amorite, as I call it, is such that where we have hitherto killed by thousands, we can now kill by hundreds of thousands."

"How horrible," exclaimed Lucia, with a shudder.

"My dear Lucia"—her father-in-law smiled thinly at her as he spoke—"the truth is never horrible, only interesting."

"But why—" asked Richard, "are you telling us all this?"

"Because I have had occasion for some time to believe that a member of this household was attempting to steal the Amorite formula. I had asked Monsieur Poirot to join us tomorrow for the weekend, so that he could take the formula back to London with him on Monday, and deliver it personally to an official at the Ministry of Defence."

"But, Claud, that's absurd. Indeed, it's highly offensive to all of us," Caroline Amory expostulated. "You can't seriously suspect—"

"I have not finished, Caroline," her

brother interrupted. "And I assure you there is nothing absurd about what I am saying. I repeat, I *had* invited Hercule Poirot to join us tomorrow, but I have had to change my plans and ask Monsieur Poirot to hurry down here from London this evening. I have taken this step because—"

Sir Claud paused. When he resumed speaking, it was more slowly, and with a much more deliberate emphasis. "Because," he repeated, as his glance swept around the assembled company, "the formula, written on an ordinary sheet of notepaper and enclosed in a long envelope, was stolen from the safe in my study sometime before dinner this evening. It was stolen by someone in this room!"

A chorus of shocked exclamations greeted the eminent scientist's announcement. Then everyone began to speak at once. "Stolen formula?" Caroline Amory began.

"What? From the safe? Impossible!" Edward Raynor exclaimed.

The babble of voices did not include that of Dr. Carelli, who remained seated, with a thoughtful expression on his face. The others, however, were silenced only when Sir Claud raised his voice and continued.

"I am in the habit of being certain of my facts," he assured his hearers. "At twenty minutes past seven exactly, I placed the formula in the safe. As I left the study, Raynor here entered it."

Blushing either from embarrassment or from anger, the secretary began, "Sir Claud, really, I must protest—"

Sir Claud raised a hand to silence him. "Raynor remained in the study," he went on, "and was still there, working, when Dr. Carelli appeared at the door. After greeting him, Raynor left Carelli alone in the study while he went to let Lucia know—"

"I protest—I—" Carelli began, but again Sir Claud raised his hand for silence, and continued his narrative. "Raynor, however," he said, "did not get further than the door of this room, where he met my sister Caroline, with Barbara. The three of them remained in this room, and Dr. Carelli joined them. Caroline and Barbara were the only two members of the party who did not enter the study."

Barbara glanced at her aunt, and then addressed Sir Claud. "I'm afraid your information about our movements isn't quite correct, Uncle Claud," she said. "I can't be excluded from your list of suspects. Do you remember, Aunt Caroline? You sent me into the study to look for a knitting needle you said you'd mislaid. You wondered if it might be in there."

Ignoring his niece's interruption, the scientist continued. "Richard came down next. He strolled into the study by himself and remained there for some minutes."

"My God!" Richard exclaimed. "Really, Father, you surely don't suspect that I'd steal your wretched formula, do you?"

Looking directly at his son, Sir Claud replied meaningfully, "That piece of paper was worth a great deal of money."

"I see." His son regarded him steadily. "And I'm in debt. That's what you mean, isn't it?"

Sir Claud made no reply to him. His gaze sweeping over the others, he continued. "As I was saying, Richard remained in the study for some minutes. He reappeared in this room just as Lucia came in. When dinner was announced, a few minutes later, Lucia was no longer with us.

I found her in the study, standing by the safe."

"Father!" exclaimed Richard, moving to his wife and putting an arm protectively about her.

"I repeat, standing by the safe," Sir Claud insisted. "She seemed very much agitated, and when I asked what was the matter she told me she felt unwell. I suggested that a glass of wine might be good for her. She assured me, however, that she was quite all right again, and then left me to join the others. Instead of following Lucia immediately to the dining-room, I remained behind in my study. I don't know why, but some instinct urged me to look in the safe. The envelope with the formula in it had disappeared."

There was a pause. No one spoke. The immense seriousness of the situation appeared to be dawning on everyone. Then Richard asked, "How have you assembled this information about our movements, Father?"

"By taking thought, of course," Sir Claud replied. "By observation and deduction. By the evidence of my own eyes, and by what I learned from questioning Tredwell."

"I notice you don't include Tredwell or any of the other servants among your suspects, Claud," Caroline Amory observed tartly. "Only your family."

"My family—and our guest," her brother corrected her. "That is so, Caroline. I have established to my own satisfaction that neither Tredwell nor any of the domestics were in the study between the time I placed the formula in the safe and the time I opened the safe again to find it missing."

He looked at each of them in turn, before adding, "I hope the position is clear to you all. Whoever took the formula must still have it. Since we returned here from dinner, the dining-room has been thoroughly searched. Tredwell would have informed me if the piece of paper had been found hidden there. And, as you now realize, I have seen to it that no one has had the opportunity to leave this room."

For some moments there was a tense silence, broken only when Dr. Carelli asked politely, "Is it your suggestion, then, Sir Claud, that we should all be searched?"

"That is not my suggestion," replied Sir Claud, consulting his watch. "It is now two minutes to nine. Hercule Poirot will have arrived at Market Cleve, where he is being met. At nine o'clock precisely, Tredwell has orders to switch off the lights from the main switch in the basement. We shall be in complete darkness in this room for one minute, and one minute only. When the lights go on again, matters will be out of my hands. Hercule Poirot will be here shortly, and he will be in charge of the case. But if, under cover of darkness, the formula is placed here"—and Sir Claud slapped his hand down on the table—"then I shall inform Monsieur Poirot that I had made a mistake and that I have no need of his services."

"That's an outrageous suggestion," Richard declared heatedly. He looked around at the others. "I say we should all be searched. I'm certainly willing."

"So am I, of course," Edward Raynor made haste to announce.

Richard Amory looked pointedly at Dr. Carelli. The Italian smiled and shrugged his shoulders. "And I."

Richard's glance moved to his aunt. "Very well, if we must, we must," Miss Amory grumbled.

"Lucia?" Richard asked, turning to his wife.

"No, no, Richard," Lucia replied breathily. "Your father's plan is best."

Richard looked at her in silence for a moment.

"Well, Richard?" queried Sir Claud.

A heavy sigh was at first his only reply, and then, "Very well, I agree." He looked at his cousin Barbara, who gave a gesture of assent.

Sir Claud leaned back in his chair wearily, and spoke in a slow, dragging voice. "The taste of that coffee is still in my mouth," he said, and then yawned.

The clock on the mantelpiece began to strike, and there was complete silence as all turned to listen. Sir Claud turned slowly in his chair and looked steadily at his son, Richard. On the last stroke of nine, the lights suddenly went out and the room was plunged into darkness.

There were a few gasps, and some stifled exclamations from the women, and then Miss Amory's voice rang out clearly. "I don't care for this at all."

"Do be quiet, Aunt Caroline," Barbara ordered her. "I'm trying to listen."

For a few seconds there was absolute silence, followed by the sounds of heavy breathing, and then a rustling of paper. Silence again, before they all heard a kind of metallic clink, the sound of something tearing, and a loud bang, which might have been a chair being knocked over.

Suddenly, Lucia screamed. "Sir Claud! Sir Claud! I can't bear it. I must have light. Somebody, please!"

The room remained in darkness. There was a sharp intake of breath, and then a loud knock at the door leading to the hall. Lucia screamed again. As though in response, the lights suddenly came on again.

Richard was now standing by the door, apparently unable to decide whether or not to attempt to open it. Edward Raynor was on his feet by his chair, which had overturned. Lucia lay back in her chair, as though about to faint.

Sir Claud sat absolutely still in his armchair, with his eyes closed. His secretary suddenly pointed to the table beside his employer. "Look," he exclaimed. "The formula."

On the table beside Sir Claud was a

long envelope of the type he had earlier described.

"Thank God!" cried Lucia. "Thank God!"

There was another knock at the door, which now opened slowly. Everyone's attention was fixed on the doorway as Tredwell ushered in a stranger and then withdrew.

The assembled company stared at the stranger.

What they saw was an extraordinary-looking little man, hardly more than five feet four inches in height, who carried himself with great dignity. His head was exactly the shape of an egg, and he carried it at a slight angle, like an inquiring terrier. His moustache was distinctly stiff and military. He was very neatly dressed.

"Hercule Poirot, at your service," said the stranger, and bowed.

Richard Amory held out a hand. "Monsieur Poirot," he said as they shook hands.

"Sir Claud?" asked Poirot. "Ah, no, you are too young, of course. You are his son, perhaps?" He moved past Richard into the centre of the room. Behind him, another man, tall, middle-aged and of military bearing, had unobtrusively entered. As he

moved to Poirot's side, the detective announced, "My colleague, Captain Hastings."

"What a delightful room," Hastings observed as he shook hands with Richard
Amory.

Richard turned back to Poirot. "I'm
sorry, Monsieur Poirot," he said, "but I fear
we have brought you down here under a
misapprehension. The need for your services has passed."

"Indeed?" replied Poirot.

"Yes, I'm sorry," Richard continued. "It's
too bad, dragging you all the way down
here from London. Of course, your fee—
and expenses—I mean—er, that'll be all
right, of course—"

"I comprehend perfectly," said Poirot,
"but for the moment it is neither my fee nor
my expenses which interests me."

"No? Then what—er—?"

"What does interest me, Mr. Amory? I
will tell you. It is just a little point, of no
consequence, of course. But it was your
father who sent for me to come. Why is it
not he who tells me to go?"

"Oh, of course. I'm sorry," said Richard,
turning towards Sir Claud. "Father, would

you please tell Monsieur Poirot that we no longer have any need of his services?"

Sir Claud did not answer.

"Father!" Richard exclaimed, moving quickly to Sir Claud's arm-chair. He bent over his father, and then turned around wildly. "Dr. Carelli," he called.

Miss Amory rose, white-faced. Carelli swiftly crossed to Sir Claud and felt his pulse. Frowning, he placed his hand over Sir Claud's heart, and then shook his head.

Poirot moved slowly to the arm-chair and stood looking down at the motionless body of the scientist. "Ye-es—I fear—" he murmured, as though to himself, "I very much fear—"

"What do you fear?" asked Barbara, moving towards him.

Poirot looked at her. "I fear that Sir Claud has sent for me too late, mademoiselle."

CHAPTER SIX

Consternation followed Hercule Poirot's statement. Dr. Carelli continued his examination of Sir Claud for a few moments before straightening himself and turning to the others. Addressing Richard Amory, "I am afraid your father is dead," he confirmed.

Richard stared at him in disbelief, as though he were unable to take the Italian doctor's words in. Then, "My God—what was it? Heart failure?" he asked.

"I—I suppose so," replied Carelli somewhat doubtfully.

Barbara moved to her aunt to comfort

her, for Miss Amory seemed about to faint. Edward Raynor joined them, helping to support Miss Amory, and whispering to Barbara as he did so, "I suppose that fellow *is* a real doctor?"

"Yes, but only an Italian one," Barbara murmured in reply, as between them they settled Miss Amory into a chair. Overhearing Barbara's remark, Poirot shook his head energetically. Then, stroking his luxuriant moustache with exquisite care, he smiled as he commented softly, "Me, I am a detective—but only a Belgian one. Nevertheless, madame, we foreigners do arrive at the correct answer occasionally."

Barbara had the grace to look at least a trifle embarrassed. She and Raynor remained in conversation for a few moments, but then Lucia approached Poirot, taking his arm and drawing him aside from the others.

"Monsieur Poirot," she urged him breathlessly, "you must stay! You must not let them send you away."

Poirot regarded her steadily. His face remained quite impassive as he asked her, "Is it that you wish me to stay, madame?"

"Yes, yes," replied Lucia, glancing anxiously towards the body of Sir Claud, still seated in its upright position in the armchair. "There's something wrong about all this. My father-in-law's heart was perfectly all right. Perfectly, I tell you. Please, Monsieur Poirot, you must find out what has happened."

Dr. Carelli and Richard Amory continued to hover near the body of Sir Claud. Richard, in an agony of indecision, appeared to be almost petrified into immobility. "I would suggest, Mr. Amory," Dr. Carelli urged him, "that you send for your father's own physician. I assume he had one?"

Richard roused himself with an effort. "What? Oh, yes," he responded. "Dr. Graham. Young Kenneth Graham. He has a practice in the village. In fact, he's rather keen on my cousin Barbara. I mean— sorry, that's irrelevant, isn't it?" Glancing across the room at Barbara, he called to her. "What's Kenneth Graham's phone number?"

"Market Cleve five," Barbara told him. Richard moved to the phone, lifted the receiver and asked for the number. While he was waiting to be connected, Edward Raynor, recalling his secretarial duties, asked

Richard, "Do you think I should order the car for Monsieur Poirot?"

Poirot spread out his hands apologetically. He was about to speak when Lucia forestalled him. "Monsieur Poirot is remaining—at my request," she announced to the company in general.

Still holding the telephone receiver to his ear, Richard turned, startled. "What do you mean?" he asked his wife tersely.

"Yes, yes, Richard, he must stay," Lucia insisted. Her voice sounded almost hysterical.

Miss Amory looked up in consternation, Barbara and Edward Raynor exchanged worried glances, Dr. Carelli stood looking down thoughtfully at the lifeless body of the great scientist, while Hastings, who had been absent-mindedly examining the books on the library shelves, turned to survey the gathering.

Richard was about to respond to Lucia's outburst when his attention was claimed by the telephone he was holding. "Oh, what . . . Is that Dr. Graham?" he asked. "Kenneth, it's Richard Amory speaking. My father has had a heart attack. Can you come up at once? . . . Well, actually, I'm afraid there's nothing to be done . . . Yes, he's dead . . . No . . . I'm afraid so . . . Thank you." Replacing the receiver, he crossed the room to his wife and, in a low, agitated voice, muttered, "Lucia, are you mad? What have you done? Don't you realize we must get rid of this detective?"

Astonished, Lucia rose from her chair. "What do you mean?" she asked Richard.

Their exchange continued quietly but urgently. "Didn't you hear what Father said?" His tone fraught with meaning, he murmured, " 'The coffee is very bitter.' "

At first, Lucia seemed not to understand. " 'The coffee is very bitter?' " she repeated. She looked at Richard uncomprehendingly for a moment, and then suddenly uttered a cry of horror which she quickly stifled.

"You see? Do you understand now?" Richard asked. Lowering his voice to a whisper, he added, "He's been poisoned. And obviously by a member of the family. You don't want a ghastly scandal, do you?"

"Oh, my God," murmured Lucia, staring straight in front of her. "Oh, merciful God."

Turning away from her, Richard approached Poirot. "Monsieur Poirot—" he began, and then hesitated.

"M'sieu?" Poirot queried politely.

Summoning up his determination, Richard continued, "Monsieur Poirot, I'm afraid I do not quite understand what it is that my wife has asked you to investigate."

Poirot considered for a moment before replying. Then, smiling pleasantly, he answered, "Shall we say, the theft of a document? That, mademoiselle tells me," he continued, gesturing towards Barbara, "is what I was called down for."

Casting a glance of reproach at Barbara, Richard told Poirot, "The document in question has been returned."

"Has it?" asked Poirot, his smile becoming rather enigmatic. The little detective suddenly had the attention of everyone present, as he moved to the table in the centre of the room and looked at the envelope still lying on it, which had been generally forgotten in the excitement and commotion caused by the discovery of Sir Claud's death.

"What do you mean?" Richard Amory asked Hercule Poirot.

Poirot gave a flamboyant twist to his

moustache and carefully brushed an imaginary speck of dust from his sleeve. Then, "It is just a—no doubt foolish—idea of mine," the little detective finally replied. "You see, someone told me the other day a most amusing story. The story of the empty bottle—there was nothing in it."

"I'm sorry, I don't understand you," Richard Amory declared.

Picking up the envelope from the table, Poirot murmured, "I just wondered . . ." He glanced at Richard, who took the envelope from him, and looked inside.

"It's empty!" Richard exclaimed. Screwing up the envelope, he threw it on the table and looked searchingly at Lucia, who moved away from him. "Then," he continued uncertainly, "I suppose we must be searched—we . . ."

Richard's voice trailed away, and he looked around the room as though seeking guidance. He was met with looks of confusion from Barbara and her aunt, indignation from Edward Raynor and blandness from Dr. Carelli. Lucia continued to avoid his eye.

"Why do you not take my advice, monsieur?" Poirot suggested. "Do nothing until the doctor comes. Tell me," he asked, pointing towards the study, "that doorway, where does he go?"

"That's my father's study in there," Richard told him. Poirot crossed the room to the door, put his head around it to look into the study, and then turned back into the library, nodding as though satisfied.

"I see," he murmured. Then, addressing Richard, he added, "*Eh bien*, monsieur. I see no need why any of you should remain in this room if you would prefer not to."

There was a general stir of relief. Dr. Carelli was the first to move. "It is understood, of course," Poirot announced, looking at the Italian doctor, "that no one should leave the house."

"I will hold myself responsible for that," Richard declared as Barbara and Raynor left together, followed by Carelli. Caroline Amory lingered by her brother's chair. "Poor dear Claud," she murmured to herself. "Poor dear Claud."

Poirot approached her. "You must have courage, mademoiselle," he told her. "The shock to you has been great, I know."

Miss Amory looked at him with tears in her eyes. "I'm so glad that I ordered the cook to prepare fried sole tonight," she said. "It was one of my brother's favorite dishes."

With a brave attempt to look serious and to match the solemnity of her delivery, Poirot answered, "Yes, yes, that must be a real comfort to you, I am sure." He shepherded Miss Amory out of the room. Richard followed his aunt out and, after a moment's hesitation, Lucia made a brisk exit. Poirot and Hastings were left alone in the room with the body of Sir Claud.

CHAPTER SEVEN

As soon as the room was empty, Hastings addressed Poirot eagerly. "Well, what do you think?" he asked.

"Shut the door, please, Hastings" was the only reply he received. As his friend complied, Poirot shook his head slowly and looked around the room. He moved about, casting an eye over the furniture and occasionally looking down at the floor. Suddenly, he stooped down to examine the overturned chair, the chair in which the secretary Edward Raynor had been sitting when the lights had gone out. From beneath the chair Poirot picked up a small object.

"What have you found?" Hastings asked him.

"A key," Poirot replied. "It looks to me as though it might be the key of a safe. I observed a safe in Sir Claud's study. Will you have the goodness, Hastings, to try this key and tell me if it fits?"

Hastings took the key from Poirot and went into the study with it. Meanwhile, Poirot approached the body of the scientist and, feeling in the trouser pocket, removed from it a bunch of keys, each of which he examined closely. Hastings returned, informing Poirot that, indeed, the key fitted the safe in the study. "I think I can guess what happened," Hastings continued. "I imagine Sir Claud must have dropped it, and—er—"

He broke off, and Poirot slowly shook his head doubtfully. "No, no, *mon ami,* give me the key, please," he requested, frowning to himself as though perplexed. He took the key from Hastings and compared it with one of the keys on the bunch. Then, putting them back in the dead scientist's pocket, he held up the single key.

"This," he told Hastings, "is a duplicate. It is, indeed, clumsily made, but no doubt it served its purpose.

In great excitement, Hastings exclaimed, "Then that means—"

He was stopped by a warning gesture from Poirot. The sound of a key being turned in the lock of the other door which led to the front hall and the staircase to the upper floors of the house was heard. As the two men turned, it opened slowly, and Tredwell, the butler, stood in the doorway.

"I beg your pardon, sir," said Tredwell as he came into the room and shut the door behind him. "The master told me to lock this door, as well as the other one leading from this room, until you arrived. The master . . ." He stopped on seeing the motionless figure of Sir Claud in the chair.

"I am afraid your master is dead," Poirot told him. "May I ask your name?"

"Tredwell, sir." The servant moved to the front of the desk, looking at the body of his master. "Oh dear. Poor Sir Claud!" he murmured. Turning to Poirot, he added, "Do please forgive me, sir, but it's such a shock. May I ask what happened? Is it— murder?"

"Why should you ask that?" said Poirot.

Lowering his voice, the butler replied, "There have been strange things happening this evening, sir."

"Oh?" exclaimed Poirot, as he exchanged glances with Hastings. "Tell me about these strange things."

"Well, I hardly know where to begin, sir," Tredwell replied. "I—I think I first felt that something was wrong when the Italian gentleman came to tea."

"The Italian gentleman?"

"Dr. Carelli, sir."

"He came to tea unexpectedly?" asked Poirot.

"Yes, sir, and Miss Amory asked him to stay for the weekend, seeing as how he was a friend of Mrs. Richard's. But if you ask me, sir—"

He stopped, and Poirot gently prompted him. "Yes?"

"I hope you will understand, sir," said Tredwell, "that it is not my custom to gossip about the family. But seeing that the master is dead . . ."

He paused again, and Poirot murmured sympathetically, "Yes, yes, I understand. I am sure you were very attached to your master." Tredwell nodded, and Poirot continued, "Sir Claud sent for me in order to tell me something. You must tell me all you can."

"Well, then," Tredwell responded, "in my opinion, sir, Mrs. Richard Amory did not want the Italian gentleman asked to dinner. I observed her face when Miss Amory gave the invitation."

"What is your own impression of Dr. Carelli?" asked Poirot.

"Dr. Carelli, sir," replied the butler rather haughtily, "is not one of us."

Not quite understanding Tredwell's remark, Poirot looked inquiringly at Hastings, who turned away to hide a smile. Throwing his colleague a glance of mild reproof, Poirot turned again to Tredwell. The butler's countenance remained perfectly serious.

"Did you feel," Poirot queried, "that there was something odd about Dr. Carelli's coming to the house in the way that he did?"

"Precisely, sir. It wasn't natural, somehow. And it was after he arrived that the trouble began, with the master telling me earlier this evening to send for you, and giving orders about the doors being locked. Mrs. Richard, too, hasn't been herself all the evening. She had to leave the dinner-table. Mr. Richard, he was very upset about it."

"Ah," said Poirot, "she had to leave the table? Did she come into this room?"

"Yes, sir," Tredwell replied.

Poirot looked around the room. His eye alighted on the handbag which Lucia had left on the table. "One of the ladies has left her bag, I see," he observed, as he picked it up.

Moving closer to him to look at the handbag, Tredwell told Poirot, "That is Mrs. Richard's, sir."

"Yes," Hastings confirmed. "I noticed her laying it down there just before she left the room."

"Just before she left the room, eh?" said Poirot. "How curious." He put the bag down on the settee, frowned perplexedly, and stood there, apparently lost in thought.

"About locking the doors, sir," Tredwell continued after a brief pause. "The master told me—"

Suddenly starting out of his reverie, Poirot interrupted the butler. "Yes, yes, I must hear all about that. Let us go through here," he suggested, indicating the door nearer to the front of the house.

Tredwell went to the door, followed by Poirot. Hastings, however, declared rather importantly, "I think I'll stay here."

Poirot turned, and regarded Hastings quizzically. "No, no, please come with us," he requested his colleague.

"But don't you think it better—" Hastings began, when Poirot interrupted him, now speaking solemnly and meaningfully. "I need your co-operation, my friend," he said.

"Oh, well, of course, in that case—"

The three men left the room together, closing the door behind them. No more than a few seconds later, the other door leading to the hallway was opened cautiously and Lucia entered surreptitiously. After a hurried glance around the room, as though to assure herself that there was no one there, she approached the round table in the centre of the room and picked up Sir Claud's coffee-cup. A shrewd, hard look came into her eyes which belied their customary innocent appearance, and she looked suddenly a good deal older.

Lucia was still standing with the cup in her hand, as though undecided what to do, when the other door leading to the front of the house opened and Poirot entered the library alone.

"Permit me, madame," said Poirot, causing Lucia to start violently. He moved across to her and took the cup from her hand with the air of one indulging in a gesture of simple politeness.

"I—I—came back for my bag," Lucia gasped.

"Ah, yes," said Poirot. "Now, let me see, where did I observe a lady's handbag? Ah yes, over here." He went to the settee, picked up the bag, and handed it to Lucia. "Thank you so much," she said, glancing around distractedly as she spoke.

"Not at all, madame."

After a brief nervous smile at Poirot, Lucia quickly left the room. When she had gone, Poirot stood quite still for a moment or two, and then picked up the coffee-cup. After smelling it cautiously, he took from his pocket a test-tube, poured some of the dregs from Sir Claud's cup into it, and sealed the tube. Replacing it in his pocket, he then proceeded to look around the room, counting the cups aloud. "One, two, three, four, five, six. Yes, six coffee-cups."

A perplexed frown was beginning to gather between Poirot's brows, when suddenly his eyes shone with that green light that always betokened inward excitement. Moving swiftly to the door through which he had recently entered, he opened it and slammed it noisily shut again, and then darted to the French windows, concealing himself behind the curtains. After a few moments the other door to the hallway opened once more, and Lucia entered again, this time even more cautiously than before, appearing to be very much on her guard. Looking about her in an attempt to keep both doors in her sight, she snatched up the coffee-cup from which Sir Claud had drunk and surveyed the entire room.

Her eye alighted on the small table near the door to the hall, on which there stood a large bowl containing a house plant. Moving to the table, Lucia thrust the coffee-cup upside down into the bowl. Then, still watching the door, she took one of the other coffee-cups and placed it near Sir Claud's body. She then moved quickly to the door, but as she reached it, the door opened and her husband Richard entered with a very tall, sandy-haired man in his early thirties, whose countenance, though amiable, had an air of authority about it. The newcomer was carrying a Gladstone bag.

"Lucia!" Richard exclaimed, startled. "What are you doing here?"

"I—I—came to get my handbag," Lucia explained. "Hello, Dr. Graham. Excuse me, please," she added, hurrying past them. As Richard watched her go, Poirot emerged from behind the curtains, approaching the two men as though he had just entered the room by the other door.

"Ah, here is Monsieur Poirot. Let me introduce you. Poirot, this is Dr. Graham. Kenneth Graham." Poirot and the doctor bowed to each other, and Dr. Graham went immediately to the body of the dead scientist to examine it, watched by Richard. Hercule Poirot, to whom they paid no further attention, moved about the room, counting the coffee-cups again with a smile. "One, two, three, four, five," he murmured. "Five, indeed." A light of pure enjoyment lit up Poirot's face, and he smiled in his most inscrutable fashion. Taking the test-tube out of his pocket, he looked at it and slowly shook his head.

Meanwhile, Dr. Graham had concluded a cursory examination of Sir Claud Amory's body. "I'm afraid," he said to Richard, "that I shan't be able to sign a death certificate. Sir Claud was in perfectly healthy condition, and it seems extremely unlikely to me that he could have suffered a sudden heart attack. I fear we shall have to find out what he had eaten or drunk in his last hours."

"Good heavens, man, is that really necessary?" asked Richard, with a note of alarm in his voice. "He hadn't eaten or drunk anything that the rest of us didn't. It's absurd to suggest—"

"I'm not suggesting anything," Dr. Graham interrupted, speaking firmly and with authority. "I'm telling you that there will have to be an inquest, by law, and that the coroner will certainly want to know the cause of death. At present I simply do not know what caused Sir Claud's death. I'll have his body removed, and I'll arrange for an autopsy to be done first thing tomorrow morning as a matter of urgency. I should be able to get back to you later tomorrow with some hard facts."

He left the room swiftly, followed by a still expostulating Richard. Poirot looked after them, and then assumed a puzzled expression as he turned to look again at the body of the man who had called him away from London with such urgency in his voice. What was it you wanted to tell me, my friend? I wonder. What did you fear? he thought to himself. "Was it simply the theft of your formula, or did you fear for your life as well? You relied on Hercule Poirot for help. You called for help too late, but I shall try to discover the truth."

Shaking his head thoughtfully, Poirot was about to leave the room when Tredwell entered. "I've shown the other gentleman to his room, sir," he told Poirot. "May I take you to yours, which is the adjoining one at the top of the stairs? I've also taken the liberty of providing a little cold supper for you both, after your journey. On the way upstairs I'll show you where the dining-room is."

Poirot inclined his head in polite acceptance. "Thank you very much, Tredwell," he said. "Incidentally, I am going to advise

Mr. Amory most strongly that this room should be kept locked until tomorrow, when we should have further information about this evening's distressing occurrence. Would you be so kind as to make it secure after we leave it now?"

"Most certainly sir, if that is your wish," replied Tredwell as Poirot preceded him out of the library.

Mr. Amory most strongly that this room should be kept locked until tomorrow, when we should have further information about this evening's distressing occurrence. Would you be so kind as to make it secure after we leave it now?"

"Most certainly sir, if that is your wish," replied Tredwell as Poirot preceded him out of the library.

CHAPTER EIGHT

When Hastings came down to breakfast late the following morning, after having slept long and well, he found himself eating alone. From Tredwell he learned that Edward Raynor had breakfasted much earlier, and had gone back to his room to put some of Sir Claud's papers in order, that Mr. and Mrs. Amory had had breakfast in their suite of rooms and had not yet appeared, and that Barbara Amory had taken a cup of coffee out into the garden, where she was presumably still sunning herself. Miss Caroline Amory had ordered breakfast in her room, pleading a slight headache, and Tredwell had not seen her subsequently.

"Have you caught sight of Monsieur Poirot at all this morning, Tredwell?" Hastings asked, and was told that his friend had risen early and had decided to take a walk to the village. "I understood Monsieur Poirot to say that he had some business to conduct there," Tredwell added.

After finishing a lavish breakfast of bacon, sausage and eggs, toast and coffee, Hastings returned to his comfortable room on the first floor, which offered a splendid view of part of the garden and, for a few minutes which Hastings found rewarding, of the sun-bathing Barbara Amory as well. It was not until Barbara had come indoors that Hastings settled down in an arm-chair with that morning's *Times,* which had of course gone to press too early to contain any mention of Sir Claud Amory's death the previous evening.

Hastings turned to the editorial page and began to read. A good half-hour later, he awakened from a light slumber to find Hercule Poirot standing over him.

"Ah, *mon cher,* you are hard at work on the case, I see," Poirot chuckled.

"As a matter of fact, Poirot, I was thinking about last night's events for quite some time," Hastings asserted. "I must have dozed off."

"And why not, my friend?" Poirot assured him. "Me, I have been thinking about the death of Sir Claud as well, and, of course, the theft of his so important formula. I have, in fact, already taken some action, and I am expecting at any minute a telephone message to tell me if a certain suspicion of mine is correct or not."

"What or whom do you suspect, Poirot?" Hastings asked eagerly.

Poirot looked out of the window before replying. "No, I do not think I can reveal that to you at this stage of the game, my friend," he replied mischievously. "Let us just say that, as the magicians on the stage like to assure us, the quickness of the hand deceives the eye."

"Really, Poirot," Hastings exclaimed, "you can be extremely irritating at times. I do think you ought to at least let me know whom you suspect of having stolen the formula. After all, I might be able to help you by—"

Poirot stopped his colleague with an airy

gesture of his hand. The little detective was now wearing his most innocent expression and gazing out of the window, meditatively, into the far distance. "You are puzzled, Hastings?" he asked. "You are wondering to yourself why I do not launch myself in pursuit of a suspect?"

"Well—something of the kind," Hastings admitted.

"It is no doubt what you would do, if you were in my place," observed Poirot complacently. "I understand that. But I am not of those who enjoy rushing about, seeking a needle in a hay-stack, as you English say. For the moment, I am content to wait. As to why I wait—*eh bien,* to the intelligence of Hercule Poirot things are sometimes perfectly clear which are not at all clear to those who are not so greatly gifted."

"Good Lord, Poirot!" Hastings exclaimed. "Do you know, I'd give a considerable sum of money to see you make a thorough ass of yourself—just for once. You're so confoundedly conceited!"

"Do not enrage yourself, my dear Hastings," Poirot replied soothingly. "In verity, I observe that there are times when you seem almost to detest me! Alas, I suffer the penalties of greatness!"

The little man puffed out his chest and sighed so comically that Hastings was forced to laugh. "Poirot, you really have the best opinion of yourself of anyone I've ever known," he declared.

"What will you? When one is unique, one knows it. But now to serious matters, my dear Hastings. Let me tell you that I have asked Sir Claud's son, Mr. Richard Amory, to meet us in the library at noon. I say 'us,' Hastings, for I need you to be there, my friend, to observe closely."

"As always, I shall be delighted to assist you, Poirot," his friend assured him.

At noon Poirot, Hastings and Richard Amory met in the library, from which the body of Sir Claud had been removed late the previous evening. While Hastings listened and observed from a comfortable position on the settee, the detective asked Richard Amory to recount in detail the events of the evening prior to his, Poirot's, arrival. When he had concluded his recital of events, Richard, sitting in the chair which his father had occupied the previous

evening, added, "Well, that's about everything, I think. I hope I've made myself
clear?"

"But perfectly, Monsieur Amory, perfectly," Poirot replied, leaning against an
arm of the only arm-chair in the room. "I
now have a clear tableau." Shutting his
eyes, he attempted to conjure up the
scene. "There is Sir Claud in his chair,
dominating the situation. Then the darkness, the knocking on the door. Yes, indeed, a dramatic little scene."

"Well," said Richard, making as if to
rise, "if that is all—"

"Just one little minute," said Poirot, with
a gesture as though to detain him.

Lowering himself to his chair again with
an air of reluctance, Richard asked,
"Yes?"

"What about earlier in the evening, Monsieur Amory?"

"Earlier in the evening?"

"Yes," Poirot reminded him. "After dinner."

"Oh, that!" said Richard. "There's really
nothing more to tell. My father and his secretary, Raynor—Edward Raynor—went

straight into my father's study. The rest of us were in here."

Poirot beamed at Richard encouragingly. "And you did—what?"

"Oh, we just talked. We had the gramophone on for most of the time."

Poirot thought for a moment. Then, "Nothing took place that strikes you as worth recalling?" he asked.

"Nothing whatever," Richard affirmed very quickly.

Watching him closely, Poirot pressed on. "When was the coffee served?"

"Immediately after dinner" was Richard's reply.

Poirot made a circular motion with his hand. "Did the butler hand it around, or did he leave it here to be poured out?"

"I really can't remember," said Richard.

Poirot gave a slight sigh. He thought for a moment, and then asked, "Did you all take coffee?"

"Yes, I think so. All except Raynor, that is. He doesn't drink coffee."

"And Sir Claud's coffee was taken to him in the study?"

"I suppose so," replied Richard, with some irritation beginning to show in his voice. "Are all these details really necessary?"

Poirot lifted his arms in a gesture of apology. "I am so sorry," he said. "It is just that I am very anxious to get the whole picture straight in my mind's eye. And, after all, we do want to get this precious formula back, do we not?"

"I suppose so" was again Richard's rather sullen rejoinder, at which Poirot's eyebrows shot up exaggeratedly and he uttered an exclamation of surprise. "No, of course, of course, we do," Richard hastened to add.

Poirot, looking away from Richard Amory, asked, "Now, when did Sir Claud come from the study into this room?"

"Just as they were trying to get that door open," Amory told him.

"They?" queried Poirot, rounding on him.

"Yes. Raynor and the others."

"May I ask who wanted it opened?"

"My wife, Lucia," said Richard. "She hadn't been feeling well all the evening."

Poirot's tone was sympathetic as he replied, "*La pauvre dame!* I hope she finds herself better this morning? There are one or two things I urgently desire to ask her."

"I'm afraid that's quite impossible," said Richard. "She's not up to seeing anyone, or answering any questions. In any case, there's nothing she could tell you that I couldn't."

"Quite so, quite so," Poirot assured him. "But women, Monsieur Amory, have a great capacity for observing things in detail. Still, doubtless your aunt, Miss Amory, will do as well."

"She's in bed," said Richard hastily. "My father's death was a great shock to her."

"Yes, I see," murmured Poirot thoughtfully. There was a pause. Richard, looking distinctly uncomfortable, rose and turned to the French windows. "Let's have some air," he announced. "It's very hot in here."

"Ah, you are like all the English," Poirot declared, smiling. "The good open air, you will not leave it in the open. No! It must be brought inside the house."

"You don't mind, I hope?" Richard asked.

"Me?" said Poirot. "No, of course not. I have adopted all the English habits. Everywhere, I am taken for an Englishman." On the settee, Hastings could not help but smile to himself. "But, pardon me, Monsieur Amory, is not that window locked by some ingenious device?"

"Yes, it is," replied Richard, "but the key to it is on my father's bunch of keys, which I have here." Taking the keys from his pocket, he moved to the French windows and undid the catch, flinging the windows open wide.

Moving away from him, Poirot sat on the stool, well away from the French windows and the fresh air, and shivered, while Richard took a deep breath of air and then stood for a moment looking out at the garden, before coming back to Poirot with the air of someone who has arrived at a decision.

"Monsieur Poirot," Richard Amory declared, "I won't beat about the bush. I know my wife begged you last night to remain, but she was upset and hysterical, and hardly knew what she was doing. I'm the person concerned, and I tell you frankly that I don't care a damn about the formula. My father was a rich man. This discovery of his was worth a great deal of money, but I don't need more than I've got, and I can't pretend to share his enthusiasm in the matter. There are explosives enough in the world already."

"I see," murmured Poirot thoughtfully.

"What I say," continued Richard, "is that we should let the whole thing drop."

Poirot's eyebrows shot up, as he made his familiar gesture of surprise. "You prefer that I should depart?" he asked. "That I should make no further investigations?"

"Yes, that's it." Richard Amory sounded uncomfortable as he half turned away from Poirot.

"But," the detective persisted, "whoever stole the formula would not do so in order to make no use of it."

"No," Richard admitted. He turned back to Poirot. "But still—"

Slowly and meaningfully, Poirot continued, "Then you do not object to the—how shall I put it—the stigma?"

"Stigma?" exclaimed Richard sharply.

"Five people—" Poirot explained to him, "five people had the opportunity of stealing the formula. Until one is proved guilty, the other four cannot be proved innocent."

Tredwell had entered the room while Poirot was speaking. As Richard began to stammer irresolutely, "I—that is—" the butler interrupted him.

"I beg your pardon, sir," he said to his employer, "but Dr. Graham is here, and would like to see you."

Clearly glad of the opportunity to escape further questioning from Poirot, Richard replied, "I'll come at once," moving to the door as he spoke. Turning to Poirot, he asked formally, "Would you excuse me, please?" as he left with Tredwell.

When the two men had departed, Hastings rose from the settee and approached Poirot, bursting with suppressed excitement. "I say!" he exclaimed. "Poison, eh?"

"What, my dear Hastings?" asked Poirot.

"Poison, surely!" Hastings repeated, nodding his head vigorously.

CHAPTER NINE

Poirot surveyed his friend with an amused twinkle in his eye. "How dramatic you are, my dear Hastings!" he exclaimed. "With what swiftness and brilliance you leap to conclusions!"

"Now then, Poirot," Hastings protested, "you can't put me off that way. You're not going to pretend that you think the old fellow died of heart disease. What happened last night positively leaps to the eye. But I must say Richard Amory can't be a very bright sort of chap. The possibility of poison doesn't seem to have occurred to him."

"You think not, my friend?" asked Poirot.

"I spotted it last night, when Dr. Graham announced that he couldn't issue a death certificate and said that there would have to be an autopsy."

Poirot gave a slight sigh. "Yes, yes," he murmured placatingly. "It is the result of the autopsy that Dr. Graham comes to announce this morning. We shall know whether you are right or not in a very few minutes." Poirot seemed to be about to say something further, but then checked himself. He moved to the mantelpiece and began to adjust the vase containing the spills used for lighting the fire.

Hastings watched him affectionately. "I say, Poirot," he laughed, "what a fellow you are for neatness."

"Is not the effect more pleasing now?" asked Poirot, as he surveyed the mantelpiece with his head on one side.

Hastings snorted. "I can't say it worried me greatly before."

"Beware!" said Poirot, shaking an admonishing finger at him. "The symmetry, it is everything. Everywhere there should be neatness and order, especially in the little grey cells of the brain." He tapped his head as he spoke.

"Oh, come on, don't leap onto your hobby-horse," Hastings begged him. "Just tell me what your precious little grey cells make of this business."

Poirot moved to the settee and sat before replying. He regarded Hastings steadily, his eyes narrowing like a cat's until they showed only a gleam of green. "If you would use your grey cells, and attempt to see the whole case clearly—as I attempt to do—you would perhaps perceive the truth, my friend," he announced smugly. "However," he continued, in a tone which suggested that he considered he was behaving with great magnanimity, "before Dr. Graham arrives, let us first hear the ideas of my friend Hastings."

"Well," Hastings began eagerly, "the key being found under the secretary's chair is suspicious."

"You think so, do you, Hastings?"

"Of course," his friend replied. "Highly suspicious. But, on the whole, I plump for the Italian."

"Ah!" Poirot murmured. "The mysterious Dr. Carelli."

"Mysterious, exactly," Hastings continued. "That's precisely the right word for him. What is he doing down here in the country? I'll tell you. He was after Sir Claud Amory's formula. He's almost certainly the emissary of a foreign government. You know the kind of thing I mean."

"I do, indeed, Hastings," Poirot responded with a smile. "After all, I do occasionally go to the cinema, you know."

"And if it turns out that Sir Claud was indeed poisoned"—Hastings was now well into his stride—"it makes Dr. Carelli more than ever the prime suspect. Remember the Borgias? Poison is a very Italian sort of crime. But what I'm afraid of is that Carelli will get away with the formula in his possession."

"He will not do that, my friend," said Poirot, shaking his head.

"How on earth can you be so sure?" Hastings inquired.

Poirot leaned back in his chair and brought the tips of his fingers together in his familiar manner. "I do not exactly know, Hastings," he admitted. "I cannot be sure, of course. But I have a little idea."

"What do you mean?"

"Where do you think that formula is now, my clever collaborator?" Poirot asked.

"How should I know?"

Poirot looked at Hastings for a moment, as though giving his friend a chance to consider the question. Then, "Think, my friend," he said encouragingly. "Arrange your ideas. Be methodical. Be orderly. That is the secret of success." When Hastings merely shook his head with a perplexed air, the detective attempted to give his colleague a clue. "There is only one place where it can be," Poirot told him.

"And where is that, for heaven's sake?" Hastings asked, with a distinct note of irritation in his voice.

"In this room, of course," Poirot announced, a triumphant Cheshire cat–like grin appearing on his face.

"What on earth do you mean?"

"But yes, Hastings. Just consider the facts. We know from the good Tredwell that Sir Claud took certain precautions to prevent the formula from being removed from this room. When he sprang his little surprise and announced our imminent arrival, it is quite certain, therefore, that the thief still had the formula on his person.

What must he do? He dare not risk having it found on him when I arrived. He can do only two things. He can return it, in the manner suggested by Sir Claud, or else he can hide it somewhere, under cover of that one minute of total darkness. Since he did not do the first, he must have done the second. *Voilà!* It is obvious to me that the formula is hidden in this room."

"By God, Poirot," Hastings exclaimed in great excitement, "I believe you're right! Let's look for it." He rose quickly, and moved to the desk.

"By all means, if it amuses you," Poirot responded. "But there is someone who will be able to find it more easily than you can."

"Oh, and who is that?" asked Hastings.

Poirot twirled his moustache with enormous energy. "Why, the person who hid it, *parbleu!*" he exclaimed, accompanying his words with the kind of gesture more suitably employed by a magician pulling a rabbit out of a hat.

"You mean that—"

"I mean," Poirot explained patiently to his colleague, "that sooner or later the thief will try to recapture his booty. One or the other of us, therefore, must constantly remain on guard—" Hearing the door being opened slowly and cautiously, he broke off and beckoned Hastings to join him by the gramophone, out of the immediate sight of anyone entering the room.

CHAPTER TEN

The door opened, and Barbara Amory entered the room cautiously. Taking a chair from near the wall, she placed it in front of the bookcase, climbed on it, and reached for the tin case containing the drugs. At that moment, Hastings suddenly sneezed, and Barbara, with a start, dropped the box. "Oh!" she exclaimed in some confusion. "I didn't know there was anyone here."

Hastings rushed forward and retrieved the box, which Poirot then took from him. "Permit me, mademoiselle," said the detective. "I am sure that is too heavy for you." He moved to the centre table and placed the tin case upon it. "It is a little collection of yours?" he asked. "The birds' eggs? The sea shells, perhaps?"

"I'm afraid it's much more prosaic, Monsieur Poirot," replied Barbara, with a nervous laugh. "Nothing but pills and powders!"

"But surely," said Poirot, "one so young, so full of health and vigour, has no need of these bagatelles?"

"Oh, it's not for me," Barbara assured him. "It's for Lucia. She's got such an awful headache this morning."

"La pauvre dame," murmured Poirot, his voice dripping with sympathy. "She sent you for these pills, then?"

"Yes," replied Barbara. "I gave her a couple of aspirin, but she wanted some real dope. I said I'd bring up the whole outfit—that is, if no one were here."

Poirot, leaning his hands on the box, spoke thoughtfully. "If no one were here. Why would that matter, mademoiselle?"

"Well, you know what it is in a place like this," Barbara explained. "Fuss, fuss, fuss! I mean, Aunt Caroline, for instance, is like a clucky old hen! And Richard's a damned nuisance and completely useless into the bargain, as men always are when you're ill."

Poirot nodded in comprehension. "I understand, I understand," he told Barbara, bowing his head as a sign that he accepted her explanation. He rubbed his fingers along the lid of the case containing the drugs, and then looked quickly at his hands. Pausing for a moment, he cleared his throat with a slightly affected sound, and then went on, "Do you know, mademoiselle, that you are very fortunate in your domestic servants?"

"What do you mean?" asked Barbara.

Poirot showed her the tin case. "See—" he pointed out, "on this box there is no speck of dust. To mount on a chair and bother to dust so high up there—not all domestics would be so conscientious."

"Yes," Barbara agreed. "I thought it odd last night that it wasn't dusty."

"You had this case of drugs down last night?" Poirot asked her.

"Yes, after dinner. It's full of old hospital stuff, you know."

"Let us have a look at these hospital drugs," suggested Poirot as he opened the box. Taking out some phials and holding them up, he raised his eyebrows exaggeratedly. "Strychnine—atropine—a very pretty little collection! Ah! Here is a tube of hyoscine, nearly empty!"

"What?" exclaimed Barbara. "Why, they were all full last night. I'm sure they were."

"Voilà!" Poirot held out a tube to her, and then replaced it in the box. "This is very curious. You say that all these little— what do you call them—phials—were full? Where exactly was this case of drugs last night, mademoiselle?"

"Well, when we took it down, we placed it on this table," Barbara informed him. "And Dr. Carelli was looking through the drugs, commenting on them and—"

She broke off as Lucia entered the room. Richard Amory's wife looked surprised to see the two men. Her pale, proud face seemed careworn in the daylight, and there was something wistful in the curve of her mouth. Barbara hastened to her. "Oh, darling, you shouldn't have got up," she told Lucia. "I was just coming up to you."

"My headache is much better, Barbara dear," Lucia replied, her eyes fixed on Poirot. "I came down because I want to speak to Monsieur Poirot."

"But, my pet, don't you think you should—"

"Please, Barbara."

"Oh, very well, you know best," said Barbara as she moved to the door, which Hastings rushed to open for her. When she had gone, Lucia moved to a chair and sat down. "Monsieur Poirot—" she began.

"I am at your service, madame," Poirot responded politely.

Lucia spoke hesitantly, and her voice trembled a little. "Monsieur Poirot," she began again, "last night I made a request to you. I asked you to stay on here. I—I begged you to do so. This morning I see that I made a mistake."

"Are you sure, madame?" Poirot asked her quietly.

"Quite sure. I was nervous last night, and overwrought. I am most grateful to you for doing what I asked, but now it is better that you should go."

"Ah, *c'est comme ça!*" Poirot murmured beneath his breath. Aloud, his response was merely a non-committal "I see, madame."

Rising, Lucia glanced at him nervously as she asked, "That is settled, then?"

"Not quite, madame," replied Poirot, taking a step towards her. "If you remember, you expressed a doubt that your father-in-law had died a natural death."

"I was hysterical last night," Lucia insisted. "I did not know what I was saying."

"Then you are now convinced," Poirot persisted, "that his death was, after all, natural?"

"Absolutely," Lucia declared.

Poirot's eyebrows rose a trifle. He looked at her in silence.

"Why do you look at me like that?" Lucia asked with alarm in her voice.

"Because, madame, it is sometimes difficult to set a dog on the scent. But once he has found it, nothing on earth will make him leave it. Not if he is a good dog. And I, madame, I, Hercule Poirot, am a very good dog!"

In great agitation, Lucia declared, "Oh! But you must, you really must go. I beg you, I implore you. You don't know what harm you may do by remaining!"

"Harm?" asked Poirot. "To you, madame?"

"To all of us, Monsieur Poirot. I can't explain further, but I beg you to accept my word that it is so. From the first moment I saw you, I trusted you. Please—"

She broke off as the door opened, and Richard, looking shocked, entered with Dr. Graham. "Lucia!" her husband exclaimed as he caught sight of her.

"Richard, what is it?" asked Lucia anxiously as she rushed to his side. "What has happened? Something new has happened, I can see it in your face. What is it?"

"Nothing, my dear," replied Richard with an attempt at reassurance in his tone. "Do you mind leaving us for a moment?"

Lucia's eyes searched his face. "Can't I—" she began, but hesitated as Richard moved to the door and opened it. "Please," he repeated.

With a final backward glance in which there was a distinct element of fear, Lucia left the room.

CHAPTER ELEVEN

Putting his Gladstone bag on the coffee-table, Dr. Graham crossed to the settee and sat. "I'm afraid this is a bad business, Monsieur Poirot," he announced to the detective.

"A bad business, you say? Yes? You have discovered what caused the death of Sir Claud?" asked Poirot.

"His death was due to poisoning by a powerful vegetable alkaloid," Graham declared.

"Such as hyoscine, perhaps?" Poirot suggested, picking up the tin case of drugs from the table.

"Why, yes, exactly." Dr. Graham sounded surprised at the detective's accurate surmise. Poirot took the case to the other side of the room, placing it on the gramophone table, and Hastings followed him there. Meanwhile, Richard Amory joined the doctor on the settee. "What does this mean, actually?" Richard asked Dr. Graham.

"For one thing, it means the involvement of the police," was Graham's prompt reply.

"My God!" exclaimed Richard. "This is terrible. Can't you possibly hush it up?"

Dr. Graham looked at Richard Amory steadily before he spoke, slowly and deliberately. "My dear Richard," he said. "Believe me, nobody could be more pained and grieved at this horrible calamity than I am. Especially since, under the circumstances, it does not seem likely that the poison could have been self-administered."

Richard paused for several seconds before he spoke. "Are you saying it was murder?" he asked in an unsteady voice.

Dr. Graham did not speak, but nodded solemnly.

"Murder!" exclaimed Richard. "What on earth are we going to do?"

Adopting a brisker, more business-like manner, Graham explained the procedure to be followed. "I have notified the coroner. The inquest will be held tomorrow at the King's Arms."

"And—you mean—the police will have to be involved? There's no way out of it?"

"There is not. Surely you must realize that, Richard?" said Dr. Graham.

Richard's tone was frantic as he began to exclaim, "But why didn't you warn me that—"

"Come on, Richard. Take a hold of yourself. I'm sure you understand that I have only taken such steps as I thought absolutely necessary," Graham interrupted him. "After all, no time should be lost in matters of this kind."

"My God!" exclaimed Richard.

Dr. Graham addressed Amory in a kindlier tone. "Richard, I know. I do understand. This has been a terrible shock to you. But there are things I must ask you about. Do you feel equal to answering a few questions?"

Richard made a visible effort to pull himself together. "What do you want to know?" he asked.

"First of all," said Graham, "what food and drink did your father have at dinner last night?"

"Let's see, we all had the same. Soup, fried sole, cutlets, and we finished off with a fruit salad."

"Now, what about drink?" continued Dr. Graham.

Richard considered for a moment before replying. "My father and my aunt drank burgundy. So did Raynor, I think. I stuck with whisky and soda, and Dr. Carelli— yes, Dr. Carelli drank white wine through- out the meal."

"Ah, yes, the mysterious Dr. Carelli," Graham murmured. "You'll excuse me, Richard, but how much precisely do you know about this man?"

Interested to hear Richard Amory's reply to this, Hastings moved closer to the two men. In answer to Dr. Graham, Richard declared, "I know nothing about him. I'd never met him, or even heard of him, until yesterday."

"But he is a friend of your wife?" asked the doctor.

"Apparently he is."

"Does she know him intimately?"

"Oh, no, he is a mere acquaintance, I gather."

Graham made a little clicking sound with his tongue, and shook his head. "You've not allowed him to leave the house, I hope?" he asked.

"No, no," Richard assured him. "I pointed out to him last night that, until this matter was cleared up—the business of the formula being stolen, I mean—it would be best for him to remain here at the house. In fact, I sent down to the inn where he had a room, and had his things brought up here."

"Didn't he make any protest at all?" Graham asked in some surprise.

"Oh, no, in fact he agreed quite eagerly."

"H'm" was Graham's only response to this. Then, looking about him, he asked, "Well now, what about this room?"

Poirot approached the two men. "The doors were locked last night by Tredwell, the butler," he assured Dr. Graham, "and the keys were given to me. Everything is exactly as it was, except that we have moved the chairs, as you see."

Dr. Graham looked at the coffee-cup on the table. Pointing to it, he asked, "Is that the cup?" He went across to the table, picked up the cup and sniffed at it. "Richard," he asked, "is this the cup your father drank from? I'd better take it. It will have to be analysed." Carrying the cup over to the coffee-table, he opened his bag.

Richard sprang to his feet. "Surely you don't think—" he began, but then broke off.

"It seems highly unlikely," Graham told him, "that the poison could have been administered at dinner. The most likely explanation is that the hyoscine was added to Sir Claud's coffee."

"I—I—" Richard tried to utter as he rose and took a step towards the doctor, but then broke off with a despairing gesture and left the room abruptly through the French windows into the garden.

Dr. Graham took a small cardboard box of cotton wool from his bag and carefully packed the cup in it, talking to Poirot as he did so. "A nasty business," he confided. "I'm not at all surprised that Richard

Amory is upset. The newspapers will make the most of this Italian doctor's friendship with his wife. And mud tends to stick, Monsieur Poirot. Mud tends to stick. Poor lady! She was probably wholly innocent. The man obviously made her acquaintance in some plausible way. They're astonishingly clever, these foreigners. Of course, I suppose I shouldn't be talking this way, as though the thing were a foregone conclusion, but what else is one to imagine?"

"You think it leaps to the eye, yes?" Poirot asked him, exchanging glances with Hastings.

"Well, after all," Dr. Graham explained, "Sir Claud's invention was valuable. This foreigner comes along, of whom nobody knows anything. An Italian. Sir Claud is mysteriously poisoned—"

"Ah, yes! The Borgias," exclaimed Poirot.

"I beg your pardon?" asked the doctor.

"Nothing, nothing."

Dr. Graham picked up his bag and prepared to leave, holding out his hand to Poirot. "Well, I'd best be off."

"Goodbye—for the present, Monsieur le Docteur," said Poirot as they shook hands.

At the door, Graham paused and looked back. "Goodbye, Monsieur Poirot. You will see that nobody disturbs anything in this room until the police arrive, won't you? That's extremely important."

"Most certainly, I shall make myself responsible for it," Poirot assured him.

As Graham left, closing the door behind him, Hastings observed drily, "You know, Poirot, I shouldn't like to be ill in this house. For one thing, there appears to be a poisoner at loose in the place—and, for another, I'm not at all sure I trust that young doctor."

Poirot gave Hastings a quizzical look. "Let us hope that we will not be in this house long enough to become ill," he said, moving to the fireplace and pressing the bell. "And now, my dear Hastings, to work," he announced as he rejoined his colleague, who was contemplating the coffee-table with a puzzled expression.

"What are you going to do?" Hastings asked.

"You and I, my friend," replied Poirot with a twinkle in his eye, "are going to interview Cesare Borgia."

Tredwell entered in response to Poirot's call. "You rang, sir?" the butler asked.

"Yes, Tredwell. Will you please ask the Italian gentleman, Dr. Carelli, if he would be kind enough to come here?"

"Certainly, sir," Tredwell replied. He left the room, and Poirot went to the table to pick up the case of drugs. "It would be well, I think," he confided to Hastings, "if we were to put this box of so very dangerous drugs back in its proper place. Let us, above all things, be neat and orderly."

Handing the tin case to Hastings, Poirot took a chair to the bookcase and climbed onto it. "The old cry for neatness and symmetry, eh?" Hastings exclaimed. "But there's more to it than that, I imagine."

"What do you mean, my friend?" asked Poirot.

"I know what it is. You don't want to scare Carelli. After all, who handled those drugs last night? Amongst others, he did. If he saw them down on the table, it might put him on his guard, eh, Poirot?"

Poirot tapped Hastings on the head. "How astute is my friend Hastings," he declared, taking the case from him.

"I know you too well," Hastings insisted. "You can't throw dust in my eyes."

As Hastings spoke, Poirot drew a finger along the top of the bookshelf, sweeping dust down into his friend's upturned face. "It seems to me, my dear Hastings, that that is precisely what I have done," Poirot exclaimed as he gingerly drew a finger along the shelf again, making a grimace as he did so. "It appears that I have praised the domestics too soon. This shelf is thick with dust. I wish I had a good wet duster in my hand to clean it up!"

"My dear Poirot," Hastings laughed, "you're not a housemaid."

"Alas, no," observed Poirot sadly. "I am only a detective!"

"Well, there's nothing to detect up there," Hastings declared, "so get down."

"As you say, there is nothing—" Poirot began, and then stopped dead, standing quite still on the chair as though turned to stone.

"What is it?" Hastings asked him impatiently, adding, "Do get down, Poirot. Dr. Carelli will be here at any minute. You don't want him to find you up there, do you?"

"You are right, my friend," Poirot agreed as he got down slowly from the chair. His face wore a solemn expression.

"What on earth is the matter?" asked Hastings.

"It is that I am thinking of something," Poirot replied with a faraway look in his eyes.

"What are you thinking of?"

"Dust, Hastings. Dust," said Poirot in an odd voice.

The door opened, and Dr. Carelli entered the room. He and Poirot greeted each other with the greatest of ceremony, each politely speaking the other's native tongue. *"Ah, Monsieur Poirot,"* Carelli began. *"Vous voulez me questionner?"*

"Sì, Signor Dottore, se Lei permette," Poirot replied.

"Ah, Lei parla italiano?"

"Sì, ma preferisco parlare in francese."

"Alors," said Carelli, *"qu'est-ce que vous voulez me demander?"*

"I say," Hastings interjected with a certain irritation in his voice. "What the devil is all this?"

"Ah, the poor Hastings is not a linguist.

I had forgotten." Poirot smiled. "We had better speak English."

"I beg your pardon. Of course," Carelli agreed. He addressed Poirot with an air of great frankness. "I am glad that you have sent for me, Monsieur Poirot," he declared. "Had you not done so, I should myself have requested an interview."

"Indeed?" remarked Poirot, indicating a chair by the table.

Carelli sat, while Poirot seated himself in the arm-chair, and Hastings made himself comfortable on the settee. "Yes," the Italian doctor continued. "As it happens, I have business in London of an urgent nature."

"Pray, continue," Poirot encouraged him.

"Yes. Of course, I quite appreciated the position last night. A valuable document had been stolen. I was the only stranger present. Naturally, I was only too willing to remain, to permit myself to be searched, in fact to insist on being searched. As a man of honour, I could do nothing else."

"Quite so," Poirot agreed. "But today?"

"Today is different," replied Carelli. "I

have, as I say, urgent business in London."

"And you wish to take your departure?"

"Exactly."

"It seems most reasonable," Poirot declared. "Do you not think so, Hastings?"

Hastings made no reply, but looked as though he did not think it at all reasonable.

"Perhaps a word from you, Monsieur Poirot, to Mr. Amory, would be in order," Carelli suggested. "I should like to avoid any unpleasantness."

"My good offices are at your disposal, Monsieur le Docteur," Poirot assured him. "And now, perhaps you can assist me with one or two details."

"I should be only too happy to do so," Carelli replied.

Poirot considered for a moment, before asking, "Is Madame Richard Amory an old friend of yours?"

"A very old friend," said Carelli. He sighed. "It was a delightful surprise, running across her so unexpectedly in this out-of-the-way spot."

"Unexpectedly, you say?" Poirot asked.

"Quite unexpectedly," Carelli replied, with a quick glance at the detective.

"Quite unexpectedly," Poirot repeated. "Fancy that!"

A certain tension had crept into the atmosphere. Carelli looked at Poirot sharply, but said nothing.

"You are interested in the latest discoveries of science?" Poirot asked him.

"Certainly. I am a doctor."

"Ah! But that does not quite follow, surely," Poirot observed. "A new vaccine, a new ray, a new germ—all this, yes. But a new explosive, surely that is not quite the province of a doctor of medicine?"

"Science should be of interest to all of us," Carelli insisted. "It represents the triumph of man over nature. Man wrings secrets from nature in spite of her bitter opposition."

Poirot nodded his head in agreement. "It is indeed admirable, what you say there. It is poetic! But, as my friend Hastings reminded me just now, I am only a detective. I appreciate things from a more practical standpoint. This discovery of Sir Claud's— it was worth a great amount of money, eh?"

"Possibly." Carelli's tone was dismissive. "I have not given that side of the matter much thought."

"You are evidently a man of lofty principles," observed Poirot, "and also, no doubt, a man of means. Travelling, for instance, is an expensive hobby."

"One should see the world one lives in," said Carelli drily.

"Indeed," Poirot agreed. "And the people who live in it. Curious people, some of them. The thief, for instance—what a curious mentality he must have!"

"As you say," Carelli agreed, "most curious."

"And the blackmailer," Poirot continued.

"What do you mean?" Carelli asked sharply.

"I said, the blackmailer," Poirot repeated. There was an awkward pause, before he continued, "But we are wandering from our subject—the death of Sir Claud Amory."

"The death of Sir Claud Amory? Why is that our subject?"

"Ah, of course," Poirot recalled. "You do not yet know. I am afraid that Sir Claud did not die as the result of a heart attack. He was poisoned." He watched the Italian closely for his reaction.

"Ah!" murmured Carelli, with a nod of the head.

"That does not surprise you?" asked Poirot.

"Frankly, no," Carelli replied. "I suspected as much last night."

"You see, then," Poirot continued, "that the matter has become much more serious." His tone changed. "You will not be able to leave the house today, Dr. Carelli."

Leaning forward to Poirot, Carelli asked, "Do you connect Sir Claud's death with the stealing of the formula?"

"Certainly," Poirot replied. "Do not you?"

Carelli spoke quickly and urgently. "Is there no one in this house, no member of this family, who desired the death of Sir Claud, quite apart from any question of the formula? What does his death mean to most of the people in this house? I will tell you. It means freedom, Monsieur Poirot. Freedom, and what you mentioned just now—money. That old man was a tyrant, and apart from his beloved work he was a miser."

"Did you observe all his last night, Monsieur le Docteur?" asked Poirot innocently.

"What if I did?" replied Carelli. "I have eyes. I can see. At least three of the people in this house wanted Sir Claud out of the way." He rose, and looked at the clock on the mantelpiece. "But that does not concern me now."

Hastings leaned forward, looking very interested, as Carelli continued, "I am vexed that I cannot keep my appointment in London."

"I am desolated, Monsieur le Docteur," said Poirot. "But what can I do?"

"Well, then, you have no further need of me?" asked Carelli.

"For the moment, no," Poirot told him.

Dr. Carelli moved to the door. "I will tell you one thing more, Monsieur Poirot," he announced, opening the door and turning back to face the detective. "There are some women whom it is dangerous to drive too far."

Poirot bowed to him politely, and Carelli returned his bow somewhat more ironically before making his exit.

CHAPTER TWELVE

When Carelli had left the room, Hastings stared after him for a few moments. "I say, Poirot," he asked finally, "what do you think he meant by that?"

Poirot shrugged his shoulders. "It was a remark of no consequence," he declared.

"But Poirot," Hastings persisted, "I'm sure Carelli was trying to tell you something."

"Ring the bell once more, Hastings" was the little detective's only response. Hastings did as he was bidden, but could not refrain from a further inquiry. "What are you going to do now?"

Poirot's reply was in his most enigmatic vein. "You will see, my dear Hastings. Patience is a great virtue."

Tredwell entered the room again with his usual respectful inquiry of "Yes, sir?" Poirot beamed at him genially. "Ah, Tredwell. Will you present my compliments to Miss Caroline Amory, and ask her if she will be good enough to allow me a few minutes of her time?"

"Certainly, sir."

"I thank you, Tredwell."

When the butler had left, Hastings exclaimed, "But the old soul's in bed. Surely you're not going to make her get up if she isn't feeling well."

"My friend Hastings knows everything! So she is in bed, yes?"

"Well, isn't she?"

Poirot patted his friend's shoulder affectionately. "That is just what I want to find out."

"But, surely—" Hastings elaborated. "Don't you remember? Richard Amory said so."

The detective regarded his friend steadily. "Hastings," he declared, "here is a man killed. And how does his family react?

With lies, lies, lies everywhere! Why does Madame Amory want me to go? Why does Monsieur Amory want me to go? Why does he wish to prevent me from seeing his aunt? What can she tell me that he does not want me to hear? I tell you, Hastings, what we have here is drama! Not a simple, sordid crime, but drama. Poignant, human drama!"

He looked as though he would have expanded on this theme had not Miss Amory entered at that moment. "Monsieur Poirot," she addressed him as she closed the door, "Tredwell tells me you wanted to see me."

"Ah yes, mademoiselle," Poirot declared as he went to her. "It is just that I would like to ask you a few questions. Will you not sit down?" He led her to a chair by the table, and she sat, looking at him nervously. "But I understood that you were prostrated, ill?" Poirot continued as he sat on the other side of the table and regarded her with an expression of anxious solicitude.

"It's all been a terrible shock, of course." Caroline Amory sighed. "Really terrible! But what I always say is, somebody must keep their head. The servants, you know, are in a turmoil. Well," she continued, speaking more quickly, "you know what servants are, Monsieur Poirot. They positively delight in funerals! They prefer a death to a wedding, I do believe. Now, dear Dr. Graham! He is so kind—such a comfort. A really clever doctor, and of course he's so fond of Barbara. I think it's a pity that Richard doesn't seem to care for him, but—what was I saying? Oh yes, Dr. Graham. So young. And he quite cured my neuritis last year. Not that I am often ill. Now, this rising generation doesn't seem to me to be at all strong. There was poor Lucia last night, having to come out from dinner feeling faint. Of course, poor child, she's a mass of nerves, and what else can you expect, with Italian blood in her veins? Though she was not so bad, I remember, when her diamond necklace was stolen—"

Miss Amory paused for breath. Poirot, while she was speaking, had taken out his cigarette-case and was about to light a cigarette, but he paused and took the opportunity to ask her, "Madame Amory's diamond necklace was stolen? When was this, mademoiselle?"

Miss Amory assumed a thoughtful expression. "Let me see, it must have been— yes, it was two months ago—just about the same time that Richard had such a quarrel with his father."

Poirot looked at the cigarette in his hand. "You permit that I smoke, madame?" he asked, and on receiving a smile and a gracious nod of assent, he took a box of matches from his pocket, lit his cigarette, and looked at Miss Amory encouragingly. When that lady made no effort to resume speaking, Poirot prompted her. "I think you were saying that Monsieur Amory quarrelled with his father," he suggested.

"Oh, it was nothing serious," Miss Amory told him. "It was only over Richard's debts. Of course, all young men have debts! Although, indeed, Claud himself was never like that. He was always so studious, even when he was a lad. Later, of course, his experiments always used up a lot of money. I used to tell him he was keeping Richard too short of money, you know. But, yes, about two months ago they had quite a scene, and what with that, and Lucia's necklace missing, and her refusing to call in the police, it was a very upsetting time. And so absurd, too! Nerves, all nerves!"

"You are sure that my smoke is not deranging you, mademoiselle?" asked Poirot, holding up his cigarette.

"Oh, no, not at all," Miss Amory assured him. "I think gentlemen *ought* to smoke."

Only now noticing that his cigarette had failed to light properly, Poirot retrieved his box of matches from the table in front of him. "Surely, it is a very unusual thing for a young and beautiful woman to take the loss of her jewels so calmly?" he asked, as he lit his cigarette again, carefully replacing two dead matches in the box, which he then returned to his pocket.

"Yes, it is odd. That's what I call it," Miss Amory agreed. "Distinctly odd! But there, she didn't seem to care a bit. Oh dear, here I am gossiping on about things which can't possibly interest you, Monsieur Poirot."

"But you interest me enormously, mademoiselle," Poirot assured her. "Tell me, when Madame Amory came out from dinner last night, feeling faint, did she go up-stairs?"

"Oh, no," replied Caroline Amory. "She came into this room. I settled her here on the sofa, and then I went back to the dining-room, leaving Richard with her. Young husbands and wives, you know, Monsieur Poirot! Not that young men are nearly so romantic as they used to be when I was a girl! Oh dear! I remember a young fellow called Aloysius Jones. We used to play croquet together. Foolish fellow—foolish fellow! But there, I'm wandering from the point again. We were talking about Richard and Lucia. A very handsome couple they make, don't you think so, Monsieur Poirot? He met her in Italy, you know—on the Italian lakes—last November. It was love at first sight. They were married within a week. She was an orphan, alone in the world. Very sad, although I sometimes wonder whether it wasn't a blessing in disguise. If she'd had a lot of foreign relations—that would be a bit trying, don't you think? After all, you know what foreigners are! They— oh!" She suddenly broke off, turning in her chair to look at Poirot in embarrassed dismay. "Oh, I do beg your pardon!"

"Not at all, not at all," murmured Poirot, with an amused glance at Hastings.

"So stupid of me," Miss Amory apologized, highly flustered. "I didn't mean—of course, it's so different in your case. *'Les braves Belges,'* as we used to say during the war."

"Please, do not concern yourself," Poirot assured her. After a pause, he continued, as though her mention of the war had reminded him, "I believe—that is—I understand that the box of drugs above the bookcase is a relic of the war. You were all examining it last night, were you not?"

"Yes, that's right. So we were."

"Now, how did that come about?" inquired Poirot.

Miss Amory considered for a moment before replying. "Now, how did it happen? Ah, yes, I remember. I said I wished I had some sal volatile, and Barbara got the box down to look through it, and then the gentlemen came in, and Dr. Carelli frightened me to death with the things he said."

Hastings began to show great interest in

the turn being taken by the discussion, and Poirot prompted Miss Amory to continue. "You mean the things Dr. Carelli said about the drugs? He looked through them and examined them thoroughly, I suppose?"

"Yes," Miss Amory confirmed, "and he held one glass tube up, something with a most innocent name—bromide, I think—which I have often taken for sea-sickness—and he said it would kill twelve strong men!"

"Hyoscine hydrobromide?" asked Poirot.

"I beg your pardon?"

"Was it hyoscine hydrobromide that Dr. Carelli was referring to?"

"Yes, yes, that was it," Miss Amory exclaimed. "How clever of you! And then Lucia took it from him, and repeated something he had said—about a dreamless sleep. I detest this modern neurotic poetry. I always say that, ever since dear Lord Tennyson died, no one has written poetry of any—"

"Oh dear," muttered Poirot.

"I beg your pardon?" asked Miss Amory.

"Ah, I was just thinking of the dear Lord Tennyson. But please go on. What happened next?"

"Next?"

"You were telling us about last night. Here, in this room—"

"Ah, yes. Well, Barbara wanted to put on an extremely vulgar song. On the gramophone, I mean. Fortunately, I stopped her."

"I see," murmured Poirot. "And this little tube that the doctor held up—was it full?"

"Oh, yes," Miss Amory replied without hesitation. "Because, when the doctor made his quotation about dreamless sleep, he said that half the tablets in the tube would be sufficient."

Miss Amory got up from her chair and moved away from the table. "You know, Monsieur Poirot," she continued as Poirot rose to join her, "I've said all along that I didn't like that man. That Dr. Carelli. There's something about him—not sincere—and so oily in manner. Of course, I couldn't say anything in front of Lucia, since he is supposed to be a friend of hers, but I did not like him. You see, Lucia is so trusting! I'm certain that the man must have wormed his way into her confidence with a view to getting asked to the house and stealing the formula."

Poirot regarded Miss Amory quizzically before he asked, "You have no doubt, then, that it was Dr. Carelli who stole Sir Claud's formula?"

Miss Amory looked at the detective in surprise. "Dear Monsieur Poirot!" she exclaimed. "Who else could have done so? He was the only stranger present. Naturally, my brother would not have liked to accuse a guest, so he made an opportunity for the document to be returned. I thought it was very delicately done. Very delicately indeed!"

"Quite so," Poirot agreed tactfully, putting a friendly arm around Miss Amory's shoulder, to that lady's evident displeasure. "Now, mademoiselle, I am going to try a little experiment in which I would like your co-operation." He removed his arm from her. "Where were you sitting last night when the lights went out?"

"There!" Miss Amory declared, indicating the settee.

"Then would you be so good as to sit there once again?"

Miss Amory moved to the settee and sat. "Now, mademoiselle," announced Poirot, "I want you to make a strong effort of the imagination! Shut your eyes, if you please."

Miss Amory did as she was asked. "That is right," Poirot continued. "Now, imagine that you are back again where you were last night. It is dark. You can see nothing. But you can hear. Throw yourself back."

Interpreting his words literally, Miss Amory flung herself backwards on the settee. "No, no," said Poirot. "I mean, throw your mind back. What can you hear? That is right, cast your mind back. Now, tell me what you hear in the darkness."

Impressed by the detective's evident earnestness, Miss Amory made an effort to do as he requested. Pausing for a moment, she then began to speak, slowly and in jerks. "Gasps," she said. "A lot of little gasps—and then the noise of a chair falling—and a metallic kind of clink—"

"Was it like this?" asked Poirot, taking a key from his pocket and throwing it down on the floor. It made no sound, and Miss Amory, after waiting for a few seconds, declared that she could hear nothing. "Well, like this, perhaps?" Poirot tried again, retrieving the key from the floor and hitting it sharply against the coffee-table.

"Why, that's exactly the sound I heard last night!" Miss Amory exclaimed. "How curious!"

"Continue, I pray you, mademoiselle," Poirot encouraged her.

"Well, I heard Lucia scream and call out to Sir Claud. And then the knocking came on the door."

"That was all? You are sure?"

"Yes, I think so—oh, wait a minute! Right at the beginning, there was a curious noise, like the tearing of silk. Somebody's dress, I suppose."

"Whose dress, do you think?" asked Poirot.

"It must have been Lucia's. It wouldn't have been Barbara's, because she was sitting right next to me, here."

"That is curious," murmured Poirot thoughtfully.

"And that really is all," Miss Amory concluded. "May I open my eyes now?"

"Oh yes, certainly, mademoiselle." As

she did so, Poirot asked her, "Who poured out Sir Claud's coffee? Was it you?"

"No," Miss Amory told him. "Lucia poured out the coffee."

"When was that, exactly?"

"It must have been just after we were talking about those dreadful drugs."

"Did Mrs. Amory take the coffee to Sir Claud herself?"

Caroline Amory paused for thought. "No—" she finally decided.

"No?" asked Poirot. "Then who did?"

"I don't know—I'm not sure—let me see, now. Oh yes, I remember! Sir Claud's coffee-cup was on the table beside Lucia's own cup. I remember that, because Mr. Raynor was carrying the cup to Sir Claud in the study, and Lucia called him back and said he had taken the wrong cup— which really was very silly, because they were both exactly the same—black, without sugar."

"So," Poirot observed, "Monsieur Raynor took the coffee to Sir Claud?"

"Yes—or, at least—no, that's right, Richard took it from him, because Barbara wanted to dance with Mr. Raynor."

"Oh! So Monsieur Amory took the coffee to his father."

"Yes, that's correct," Miss Amory confirmed.

"Ah!" exclaimed Poirot. "Tell me, what had Monsieur Amory been doing just before that? Dancing?"

"Oh, no," Miss Amory replied. "He had been packing away the drugs. Putting them all back in the box tidily, you know."

"I see, I see. Sir Claud, then, drank his coffee in his study?"

"I suppose he began to do so," Miss Amory remembered. "But he came back in here with the cup in his hand. I remember his complaining about the taste, saying that it was bitter. And I assure you, Monsieur Poirot, it was the very best coffee. A special mixture that I had ordered myself from the Army and Navy Stores in London. You know, that wonderful department store in Victoria Street. It's so convenient, not far from the railway station. And I—"

She broke off as the door opened and Edward Raynor entered. "Am I interrupting?" the secretary asked. "I am so sorry. I wanted to speak to Monsieur Poirot, but I can come back later."

"No, no," declared Poirot. "I have finished putting this poor lady upon the rack!"

Miss Amory rose. "I'm afraid I haven't been able to tell you anything useful," she apologized, as she went to the door.

Poirot rose and walked ahead of her. "You have told me a great deal, mademoiselle. More than you realize, perhaps," he assured Miss Amory as he opened the door for her.

CHAPTER THIRTEEN

After seeing Miss Amory out, Poirot turned his attention to Edward Raynor. "Now, Monsieur Raynor," he said as he gestured the secretary to a chair, "let me hear what you have to tell me."

Raynor sat down and regarded Poirot earnestly. "Mr. Amory has just told me the news about Sir Claud. The cause of his death, I mean. This is a most extraordinary business, monsieur."

"It has come as a shock to you?" asked Poirot.

"Certainly. I never suspected such a thing."

Approaching him, Poirot handed Raynor the key that he had found, watching the secretary keenly as he did so. "Have you ever seen this key before, Monsieur Raynor?" he asked.

Raynor took the key and turned it about in his hands with a puzzled air. "It looks rather like the key of Sir Claud's safe," he observed. "But I understand from Mr. Amory that Sir Claud's key was in its proper place on his chain." He handed the key back to Poirot.

"Yes, this is a key to the safe in Sir Claud's study, but it is a duplicate key," Poirot told him, adding slowly and with emphasis "a duplicate which was lying on the floor beside the chair you occupied last night."

Raynor looked at the detective unflinchingly. "If you think it was I who dropped it, you are mistaken," he declared.

Poirot regarded him searchingly for a moment, and then nodded his head as if satisfied. "I believe you," he said. Moving briskly to the settee, he sat and rubbed his hands together. "Now, let us get to work, Monsieur Raynor. You were Sir Claud's confidential secretary, were you not?"

"That is correct."

"Then you knew a lot about his work?"

"Yes. I have a certain amount of scientific training, and I occasionally helped him with his experiments."

"Do you know anything," asked Poirot, "that can throw light upon this unfortunate affair?"

Raynor took a letter from his pocket. "Only this," he replied as he rose, moved across to Poirot and handed him the letter. "One of my tasks was to open and sort out all of Sir Claud's correspondence. This came two days ago."

Poirot took the letter and read it aloud. " 'You are nourishing a viper in your bosom.' Bosom?" he queried, turning to Hastings before continuing, " 'Beware of Selma Goetz and her brood. Your secret is known. Be on your guard.' It is signed 'Watcher.' H'm, very picturesque and dramatic. Hastings, you will enjoy this," Poirot remarked, passing the letter to his friend.

"What I would like to know," declared Edward Raynor, "is this. Who is Selma Goetz?"

Leaning back and putting his fingertips together, Poirot announced, "I think I can satisfy your curiosity, monsieur. Selma Goetz was the most successful international spy ever known. She was also a very beautiful woman. She worked for Italy, for France, for Germany, and eventually, I believe, for Russia. Yes, she was an extraordinary woman, Selma Goetz."

Raynor stepped back a pace, and spoke sharply. "Was?"

"She is dead," Poirot declared. "She died in Genoa, last November." He retrieved the letter from Hastings, who had been shaking his head over it with a perplexed expression.

"Then this letter must be a hoax," Raynor exclaimed.

"I wonder," Poirot murmured. " 'Selma Goetz and her brood,' it says. Selma Goetz left a daughter, Monsieur Raynor, a very beautiful girl. Since her mother's death she has disappeared completely." He put the letter in his pocket.

"Could it be possible that—?" Raynor began, then paused.

"Yes? You were going to say something, monsieur?" Poirot prompted him.

Moving to the detective, Raynor spoke eagerly. "Mrs. Amory's Italian maid. She brought her from Italy with her, a very pretty girl. Vittoria Muzio, her name is. Could she possibly be this daughter of Selma Goetz?"

"Ah, it is an idea, that." Poirot sounded impressed.

"Let me send her to you," Raynor suggested, turning to go.

Poirot rose. "No, no, a little minute. Above all, we must not alarm her. Let me speak to Madame Amory first. She will be able to tell me something about this girl."

"Perhaps you are right," Raynor agreed. "I'll tell Mrs. Amory at once."

The secretary left the room with the air of a determined man, and Hastings approached Poirot in great excitement. "That's it, Poirot! Carelli and the Italian maid in collusion, working for a foreign government. Don't you agree?"

Deep in thought, Poirot paid his colleague no heed.

"Poirot? Don't you think so? I said, it must be Carelli and the maid working together."

"Ah, yes, that is exactly what you would say, my friend."

Hastings looked affronted. "Well, what is

your idea?" he asked Poirot in an injured tone.

"There are several questions to be answered, my dear Hastings. Why was Madame Amory's necklace stolen two months ago? Why did she refuse to call in the police on that occasion? Why—?"

He broke off as Lucia Amory entered the room, carrying her handbag. "I understand you wanted to see me, Monsieur Poirot. Is that correct?" she asked.

"Yes, madame. I would like simply to ask you a few questions." He indicated a chair by the table. "Won't you sit down?"

Lucia moved to the chair and sat, as Poirot turned to Hastings. "My friend, the garden outside that window is very fine," Poirot observed, taking Hastings by the arm and propelling him gently towards the French windows. Hastings looked distinctly reluctant to leave, but Poirot's insistence, though gentle, was firm. "Yes, my friend. Observe the beauties of nature. Do not ever lose a chance of observing the beauties of nature."

Somewhat unwillingly, Hastings allowed himself to be bundled out of doors. Then, the day being warm and sunny, he decided to make the best of his present situation and explore the Amorys' garden. Ambling across the lawn, he made his way towards a hedge beyond which a formal garden looked extremely inviting.

As he walked along the length of the hedge, Hastings became aware of voices quite close by, voices which, as he approached, he recognized as those of Barbara Amory and Dr. Graham, who were, it seemed, enjoying a *tête-à-tête* on a bench, just the other side of the hedge. In the hope that he might overhear something relevant to Sir Claud Amory's death or the disappearance of the formula that would be useful for Poirot to know, Hastings stopped to listen.

"—perfectly clear that he thinks his beautiful young cousin can do better for herself than a country doctor. That seems to be the basis of his lack of enthusiasm for our seeing each other," Kenneth Graham was saying.

"Oh, I know Richard can be an old stick-in-the-mud at times, and carry on like someone twice his age," Barbara's voice replied. "But I don't think you ought to allow yourself to be affected by it, Kenny. I certainly don't take any notice of him."

"Well, I shan't either," said Dr. Graham. "But look here, Barbara, I asked you to meet me out here because I wanted to talk to you privately, without being seen or heard by the family. First of all, I ought to tell you that there can be no doubt about it, your uncle was poisoned last night."

"Oh, yes?" Barbara sounded bored.

"You don't seem at all surprised to hear that."

"Oh, I suppose I'm surprised. After all, members of one's family don't get poisoned every day, do they? But I have to admit that I'm not particularly upset that he's dead. In fact, I think I'm glad."

"Barbara!"

"Now, don't you start pretending you're surprised to hear that, Kenny. You've listened to me going on about the mean old so-and-so on countless occasions. He didn't really care for any of us, he was only interested in his mouldy old experiments. He treated Richard very badly, and he wasn't particularly welcoming to Lucia when Richard brought her back from Italy as his bride. And Lucia is so sweet, and so absolutely right for Richard."

"Barbara, darling, I have to ask you this. Now, I promise that anything you say to me will go no further. I'll protect you if necessary. But tell me, do you know something—anything at all—about your uncle's death? Have you any reason to suspect that Richard, for example, might have felt so desperate about his financial situation that he would think of killing his father in order to get his hands now on what would eventually be his inheritance?"

"I don't want to continue this conversation, Kenny. I thought you asked me out here to whisper sweet nothings to me, not to accuse my cousin of murder."

"Darling, I'm not accusing Richard of anything. But you must admit there's something wrong here. Richard doesn't seem to want a police investigation into his uncle's death. It's almost as though he were afraid of what it might reveal. There's no way he can stop the police from taking over, of course, but he's made it perfectly clear that he's furious with me for having instigated an official investigation. I was only doing my duty as a doctor, after all.

How could I possibly have signed a death certificate stating that Sir Claud had died of a heart attack? For heaven's sake, there was absolutely nothing wrong with his heart when I last gave him a regular check-up only a few weeks ago."

"Kenny, I don't want to hear any more. I'm going indoors. You'll make your own way out through the garden, won't you? I'll see you around."

"Barbara, I only want—" But she had already gone, and Dr. Graham emitted a deep sigh that was almost a groan. At that moment, Hastings thought it expedient to retrace his steps quickly back to the house without being seen by either of them.

CHAPTER FOURTEEN

Back in the library, it was only after Hastings, propelled by Hercule Poirot, had made his unwilling exit into the garden that the little detective turned his attention again to Lucia Amory, first taking care to close the French windows.

Lucia looked at Poirot anxiously. "You want to ask me about my maid, I understand, Monsieur Poirot. That is what Mr. Raynor told me. But she is a very good girl. I am sure there is nothing wrong with her."

"Madame," Poirot replied, "it is not

about your maid that I wish to speak to you."

Lucia sounded startled as she began, "But Mr. Raynor said—"

Poirot interrupted her. "I am afraid I allowed Mr. Raynor to think so for reasons of my own."

"Well, what is it then?" Lucia's voice was guarded now.

"Madame," Poirot observed, "you paid me a very pretty compliment yesterday. You said that, when you first saw me—you said—that you trusted me."

"Well?"

"Well, madame, I ask you to trust me now!"

"What do you mean?"

Poirot observed her solemnly. "You have youth, beauty, admiration, love—all the things a woman wants and craves. But there is one thing, madame, that you lack— a father confessor! Let Papa Poirot offer himself for the post."

Lucia was about to speak when Poirot interrupted her. "Now, think well before you refuse, madame. It was at your request that I remained here. I stayed to serve you. I still wish to serve you."

With a sudden flash of temperament, Lucia replied, "You can serve me best now by going, monsieur."

"Madame," Poirot continued imperturbably, "do you know that the police have been called in?"

"The police?"

"Yes."

"But by whom? And why?"

"Dr. Graham and the other doctors, his colleagues," Poirot told her, "have discovered that Sir Claud Amory was poisoned."

"Ah, no! No! Not that!" Lucia sounded more horrified than surprised.

"Yes. So you see, madame, there is very little time for you to decide on the most prudent course of action. At present, I serve you. Later, I may have to serve justice."

Lucia's eyes searched Poirot's face as though trying to decide whether to confide in him. At last, "What do you want me to do?" she asked falteringly.

Poirot sat and faced her. "What will you?" he murmured to himself, and then, addressing Lucia, he suggested gently, "Why not simply tell me the truth, madame?"

Lucia paused. Stretching out her hand towards him, she began, "I—I—" She paused again, irresolutely, and then her expression hardened. "Really, Monsieur Poirot, I am at a loss to understand you."

Poirot eyed her keenly. "Ah! It is to be like that, is it? I am very sorry."

Her composure somewhat regained, Lucia spoke coldly. "If you will tell me what you want with me, I will answer any questions you wish to ask."

"So!" the little detective exclaimed. "You pit your wits against Hercule Poirot, do you? Very well, then. Be assured, however, madame, that we shall get at the truth just the same." He tapped the table. "But by a less pleasant process."

"I have nothing to conceal," Lucia told him defiantly.

Taking from his pocket the letter Edward Raynor had given him, Poirot handed it to Lucia. "A few days ago, Sir Claud received this anonymous letter," he informed her.

Lucia glanced through the letter, apparently unmoved. "Well, what of it?" she commented as she handed it back to Poirot.

"Have you ever heard the name Selma Goetz, before?"

"Never! Who is she?" asked Lucia.

"She died—in Genoa—last November," said Poirot.

"Indeed?"

"Perhaps you met her there," Poirot remarked, replacing the letter in his pocket. "In fact, I think you did."

"I was never in Genoa in my life," Lucia insisted sharply.

"Then, if anyone were to say that they had seen you there?"

"They would—they would be mistaken."

Poirot persisted. "But I understand, madame, that you first met your husband in Genoa?"

"Did Richard say that? How stupid of him! We met first in Milan."

"Then the woman you were with in Genoa—"

Lucia interrupted him angrily. "I tell you, I was never in Genoa!"

"Ah, pardon!" exclaimed Poirot. "Of course, you said so just now. Yet it is odd!"

"What is odd?"

Poirot closed his eyes and leaned back in his chair. His voice came purringly from between his lips. "I will tell you a little story, madame," he announced, taking out a pocket-book. "I have a friend who does the photography for certain London journals. He takes—how do you say?—the snapshots of contessas and other fashionable ladies who bathe themselves on fashionable beaches. That sort of thing." Poirot searched in the pocket-book before continuing, "Last November, this friend of mine, he finds himself in Genoa, and he recognizes a very notorious lady. The Baronne de Giers, she calls herself at this time, and she is the *chère amie* of a very noted French diplomat. The world talks, but that does not matter to the lady, because the diplomat, he talks also, and that is what she wants. He is more amorous than discreet, you understand—" Poirot broke off with an innocent air. "I do not bore you, I hope, madame?"

"Not at all, but I hardly see the point of this story."

Looking through the contents of his pocket-book, Poirot continued. "I am arriving at the point, I assure you, madame. My friend, he shows me a snapshot he has taken. We agree with each other that the

Baronne de Giers is *une très belle femme,* and we are not at all surprised at the behavior of the diplomat."

"Is that all?"

"No, madame. You see, the lady was not alone. She was photographed walking with her daughter, and that daughter, madame, had a very beautiful face, and one, moreover, that it would not be at all easy to forget." Poirot rose, made his most gallant bow, and closed his pocket-book. "Of course, I recognized that face as soon as I arrived here."

Lucia looked at Poirot and drew her breath in sharply. "Oh!" she exclaimed. After a moment, she pulled herself together, and laughed. "My dear Monsieur Poirot, what a curious mistake. Of course, I see the point of all your questions now. I remember the Baronne de Giers perfectly, and her daughter as well. The daughter was rather a dull girl, but the mother fascinated me. I was quite romantic about her, and went out walking with her on several occasions. I think my devotion amused her. That was doubtless how the mistake arose. That is how someone thought that I must be the woman's daughter." Lucia sank back in her chair.

Poirot nodded slow appreciation, at which Lucia appeared visibly to relax. Then suddenly, leaning over the table towards her, the detective remarked, "But I thought you had never been to Genoa."

Taken unawares, Lucia gasped. She stared at Poirot as he put his pocket-book back in an inner pocket of his jacket. "You have no photograph," she said. It was half question, half statement.

"No," Poirot confessed. "I have no photograph, madame. I knew the name that Selma Goetz passed under in Genoa. The rest—my friend and his photography—all of that was a harmless little invention of mine!"

Lucia leaped to her feet, her eyes blazing with anger. "You set a trap for me!" she exclaimed furiously.

Poirot shrugged his shoulders. "Yes, madame," he affirmed. "I fear I had no alternative."

"What has all this to do with Sir Claud's death?" Lucia muttered as though to herself, looking wildly about the room.

Poirot affected a tone of indifference as,

instead of answering, he posed another question. "Madame," he asked, brushing an imaginary speck of dust from his jacket as he spoke, "is it true that you lost a valuable diamond necklace a little time ago?"

Lucia glared at him. "Again I ask," her words emerging as though through clenched teeth, "what has that to do with Sir Claud's death?"

Poirot spoke slowly and deliberately. "First a stolen necklace—then a stolen formula. Both would bring in a very large sum of money."

"What do you mean?" Lucia gasped.

"I mean, madame, that I would like you to answer this question. How much did Dr. Carelli want—this time?"

Lucia turned away from Poirot. "I—I—I will not answer any more questions," she whispered.

"Because you are afraid?" asked Poirot, moving to her.

Lucia turned to face him again, flinging her head back in a gesture of defiance. "No," she asserted, "I'm not afraid. I simply don't know what you are talking about! Why should Dr. Carelli ask me for money?"

"To buy his silence," Poirot replied. "The Amorys are a proud family, and you would not have wanted them to know that you are—the daughter of Selma Goetz!"

Lucia glared at Poirot for a moment without replying, and then, her shoulders sagging, she collapsed onto a chair, resting her head in her hands. At least a minute elapsed before she looked up with a sigh. "Does Richard know?" she murmured.

"He does not know yet, madame," Poirot replied slowly.

Lucia sounded desperate as she pleaded, "Don't tell him, Monsieur Poirot! Please don't tell him! He is so proud of his family name, so proud of his honour! I was wicked to have married him! But I was so miserable. I hated that life, that awful life I was forced to live with my mother. I felt degraded by it. But what could I do? And then, when Mama died, I was at last free! Free to be honest! Free to get away from that life of lies and intrigue. I met Richard. That was the most wonderful thing that had ever happened to me. Richard came into my life. I loved him, and he wanted to marry me. How could I tell him who I was? Why should I tell him?"

"And then," Poirot prompted her gently, "Carelli recognized you somewhere with Monsieur Amory, and began to blackmail you?"

"Yes, but I had no money of my own," Lucia gasped. "I sold the necklace and paid him. I thought that was the end of it all. But yesterday he turned up here. He had heard of this formula that Sir Claud had invented."

"He wanted you to steal it for him?"

Lucia sighed. "Yes."

"And did you?" asked Poirot, moving closer to her.

"You won't believe me—now," murmured Lucia, shaking her head sorrowfully.

Poirot contemplated the beautiful young woman with a look of sympathy. "Yes, yes, my child," he assured her. "I will still believe you. Have courage, and trust Papa Poirot, yes? Just tell me the truth. Did you take Sir Claud's secret formula?"

"No, no, I didn't, I didn't!" Lucia declared vehemently. "But it's true that I meant to. Carelli made a key of Sir Claud's safe from an impression I took."

Taking a key from his pocket and showing it to her, Poirot asked, "Is this it?"

Lucia looked at the key. "Yes, it was all quite easy. Carelli gave me that key. I was in the study, just steeling myself to open the safe when Sir Claud came in and found me. That's the truth, I swear it!"

"I believe you, madame," said Poirot. He returned the key to his pocket, moved to the arm-chair and sat, placing the tips of his fingers together, and pondering for a moment. "And yet you acquiesced eagerly in Sir Claud's scheme of plunging the room into darkness?"

"I didn't want to be searched," Lucia explained. "Carelli had passed me a note at the same time as the key, and they were both in my dress."

"What did you do with them?" Poirot asked her.

"When the lights went out, I threw the key as far from me as I could. Over there." She pointed in the direction of the chair in which Edward Raynor had sat on the previous evening.

"And the note that Carelli had passed to you?" Poirot continued.

"I didn't know what to do with the note."

Lucia rose and went to the table. "So I slipped it between the leaves of a book." Taking a book from the table, she searched in it. "Yes, it is still here," she declared as she removed a piece of paper from the book. "Do you wish to see it?"

"No, madame, it is yours," Poirot assured her.

Sitting in a chair by the table, Lucia tore the note into small pieces which she put in her handbag. Poirot watched her, but paused before asking, "One little thing more, madame. Did you, by any chance, tear your dress last night?"

"I? No!" Lucia sounded surprised.

"During those moments of darkness," asked Poirot, "did you hear the sound of a dress tearing?"

Lucia considered for a few seconds. Then, "Yes, now that you mention it," she said, "I believe I did. But it was not mine. It must have been Miss Amory's or Barbara's."

"Well, we will not worry about that," remarked Poirot dismissively. "Now, let us pass on to something else. Who poured out Sir Claud's coffee last night?"

"I did."

"And you put it down on that table, beside your own cup?"

"Yes."

Poirot rose, leaned forward over the table towards Lucia, and suddenly shot his next question at her. "Into which cup did you put the hyoscine?"

Lucia looked at him wildly. "How did you know?" she gasped.

"It is my business to know things. Into which cup, madame?"

Lucia sighed. "My own."

"Why?"

"Because I wanted—I wanted to die. Richard suspected that there was something between Carelli and me—that we were having an affair. He could not have been further from the truth. I hated Carelli! I hate him now. But, as I had failed to obtain the formula for him, I was sure he would expose me to Richard. To kill myself was a way out—the only way. A swift, dreamless sleep—and no awakening— that's what he said."

"Who said that to you?"

"Dr. Carelli."

"I begin to see—I begin to see," said Poirot slowly. He pointed to the cup on the table. "This is your cup, then? A full cup, untasted?"

"Yes."

"What made you change your mind about drinking it?"

"Richard came over to me. He said that he would take me away—abroad—that he would get the money to do so, somehow. He gave me back—hope."

"Now, listen to me carefully, madame," said Poirot gravely. "This morning, Dr. Graham took away the cup that was beside Sir Claud's chair."

"Yes?"

"His fellow-doctors will have found nothing but the dregs of coffee in it—" He paused.

Without looking at him, Lucia answered, "Of—of course."

"That is correct, yes?" Poirot persisted.

Lucia looked straight ahead of her without replying. Then, looking up at Poirot, she exclaimed, "Why are you staring at me like that? You frighten me!"

"I said," Poirot repeated, "that they took away the cup that was beside Sir Claud's chair this morning. Let us suppose instead that they had taken away the cup that was by his chair last night?" He moved to the table on which the plant bowl stood and took a coffee-cup from the bowl. "Let us suppose that they had taken this cup!"

Lucia rose quickly, putting her hands up to her face. "You know!" she gasped.

Poirot moved to her. "Madame!" His voice now was stern. "They will test their cup, if they have not already done so, and they will find—nothing. But last night I took some of the dregs from the original cup. What would you say if I were to tell you that there was hyoscine in Sir Claud's cup?"

Lucia looked stricken. She swayed, but then recovered herself. For a moment she said nothing. Then, "You are right," she whispered. "You are quite right. I killed him." Her voice rang out suddenly. "I killed him! I put the hyoscine in *his* cup." Going to the table, she grasped the full cup of coffee. "This one—is only coffee!"

She raised the full cup to her lips, but Poirot sprang forward, interposing his hand between the cup and her lips. They looked at each other intently for a time, then Lucia burst into sobs. Poirot took the cup from her and placed it on the table. "Madame!" he exclaimed.

"Why did you stop me?" Lucia murmured.

"Madame," Poirot told her, "the world is very beautiful. Why should you wish to leave it?"

"I—Oh!" Lucia collapsed onto the settee, sobbing bitterly.

When Poirot spoke, his voice was warm and gentle. "You told me the truth. You put the hyoscine in your own cup. I believe you. But there was hyoscine in the other cup as well. Now, speak the truth to me again. Who put the hyoscine in Sir Claud's cup?"

Lucia stared at Poirot in terror. "No, no, you're wrong. He didn't. I killed him," she cried hysterically.

"Who didn't? Whom are you shielding, madame? Tell me," Poirot demanded.

"He didn't, I tell you," Lucia sobbed.

There was a knock at the door. "That will be the police!" declared Poirot. "We have very little time. I will make you two promises, madame. Promise number one is that I will save you—"

"But I killed him, I tell you." Lucia's voice was almost at screaming pitch.

"Promise number two," Poirot continued imperturbably, "is that I will save your husband!"

"Oh!" Lucia gasped, gazing at him in bewilderment.

The butler, Tredwell, entered the room. Addressing Poirot, he announced, "Inspector Japp, from Scotland Yard."

CHAPTER FIFTEEN

Fifteen minutes later Inspector Japp, accompanied by Johnson, a young constable, had finished his initial inspection of the library. Japp, a bluff, hearty, middle-aged man with a thick-set figure and a ruddy complexion, was reminiscing with Poirot and Hastings, who had returned from his exile in the garden.

"Yes," Japp told his constable, "Mr. Poirot and I go back a long way. You've heard me speak often of him. He was still a member of the Belgian police force when we first worked together. It was the Abercrombie forgery case, wasn't it, Poirot?

We ran him down in Brussels. Ah, those were great days. And do you remember 'Baron' Altara? There was a pretty rogue for you! He eluded the clutches of half the police in Europe. But we nailed him in Antwerp—thanks to Mr. Poirot here."

Japp turned from Johnson to Poirot. "And then we met again in this country, didn't we, Poirot?" he exclaimed. "You'd retired by then, of course. You solved that mysterious affair at Styles, remember? The last time we collaborated on a case was about two years ago, wasn't it? That affair of the Italian nobleman in London. Well, it's really good to see you again, Poirot. You could have knocked me down with a feather when I came in a few minutes ago and saw your funny old mug."

"My mug?" asked Poirot, looking puzzled. English slang never failed to mystify him.

"Your face, I mean, old chap," Japp explained with a grin. "Well, shall we work together on this?"

Poirot smiled. "My good Japp, you know my little weaknesses!"

"Secretive old beggar, aren't you?" remarked Japp, smacking Poirot on the shoulder. "I say, that Mrs. Amory you were talking to when I came in, she's a good-looker. Richard Amory's wife, I suppose? I'll bet you were enjoying yourself, you old dog!"

The inspector gave a rather coarse laugh and seated himself on a chair by the table. "Anyway," he continued, "this is just the sort of case that suits you down to the ground. It pleases your tortuous mind. Now, I loathe a poisoning case. Nothing to go on. You have to find out what they ate and drank, and who handled it, and who so much as breathed on it! I admit Dr. Graham seems pretty clear on the case. He says the dope must have been in the coffee. According to him, such a large dose would have been almost instantaneous in effect. Of course, we shall know for certain when we get the analyst's report, but we've got enough to go on."

Japp rose to his feet. "Well, I've finished with this room," he declared. "I'd better have a few words with Mr. Richard Amory, I suppose, and then I'll see this Dr. Carelli. It looks as though he's our man. But keep an open mind, that's what I always say, keep an open mind." He moved to the door. "Coming, Poirot?"

"But certainly, I will accompany you," said Poirot, joining him.

"Captain Hastings too, I've no doubt." Japp laughed. "Sticks as close to you as your shadow, doesn't he, Poirot?"

Poirot threw a meaningful glance at his friend. "Perhaps Hastings would prefer to remain here," he remarked.

Taking his cue in a somewhat obvious manner, Hastings replied, "Yes, yes, I think I'll stay here."

"Well, as you please." Japp sounded surprised. He and Poirot left, followed by the young constable, and a moment later Barbara Amory entered from the garden through the French windows, wearing a pink blouse and light-coloured slacks. "Ah! There you are, my pet. I say, what's this that's just blown in upon us?" she asked Hastings, as she moved across to the settee and sat down. "Is it the police?"

"Yes," Hastings told her. He joined her on the settee. "It's Inspector Japp of Scotland Yard. He's gone to see your cousin now, to ask him a few questions."

"Will he want to ask me questions, do you think?"

"I don't imagine so. But even if he does," Hastings assured her, "there's nothing to be alarmed about."

"Oh, I'm not alarmed," Barbara declared. "In fact, I think it would be absolutely wizard! But it would be so tempting to embroider a bit, just to make a sensation. I adore sensation, don't you?"

Hastings looked puzzled. "I—I really don't know. No, I don't think I adore sensation."

Barbara Amory regarded him quizzically. "You know, you intrigue me," she declared. "Where have you been all your life?"

"Well, I've spent several years in South America."

"I knew it!" Barbara exclaimed. She gestured, with her hand over her eyes. "The wide-open spaces. That's why you're so deliciously old-fashioned."

Hastings now looked offended. "I'm sorry," he said stiffly.

"Oh, but I adore it," Barbara hastened to explain. "I think you're a pet, an absolute pet."

"What exactly do you mean by old-fashioned?"

"Well," Barbara continued, "I'm sure you believe in all sorts of stuffy old things, like decency, and not telling lies except for a very good reason, and putting a good face on things."

"Quite," agreed Hastings in some surprise. "Don't you?"

"Me? Well, for example, do you expect me to keep up the fiction that Uncle Claud's death is a regrettable incident?"

"Isn't it?" Hastings sounded shocked.

"My dear!" exclaimed Barbara. She rose and perched herself on the edge of the coffee-table. "As far as I'm concerned, it's the most marvellous thing that ever happened. You don't know what an old skinflint he was. You don't know how he ground us all down!" She stopped, overcome by the strength of her feelings.

Embarrassed, Hastings began, "I—I— wish you wouldn't—" but was interrupted by Barbara. "You don't like honesty?" she asked. "That's just what I thought you'd be like. You'd prefer me to be wearing black instead of this, and to be talking in a hushed voice about 'Poor Uncle Claud! So good to us all.' "

"Really!" Hastings exclaimed.

"Oh, you needn't pretend," Barbara went on, "I knew that's what you'd turn out to be like, if I got to know you properly. But what I say is that life isn't long enough for all that lying and pretence. Uncle Claud wasn't good to us at all. I'm certain we're all glad he's dead, really, in our heart of hearts. Yes, even Aunt Caroline. Poor dear, she's stood him longer than any of us."

Barbara suddenly calmed down. When she spoke again, it was in a milder tone. "You know, I've been thinking. Scientifically speaking, Aunt Caroline might have poisoned Uncle Claud. That heart attack last night was really very queer. I don't believe it was a heart attack at all. Just suppose that suppressing her feelings all these years had led to Aunt Caroline developing some powerful complex—"

"I suppose it's theoretically possible," Hastings murmured guardedly.

"I wonder who pinched the formula, though," Barbara continued. "Everyone says it was the Italian, but personally I suspect Tredwell."

"Your butler? Good heavens! Why?"

"Because he never went near the study!"

Hastings looked perplexed. "But then—"

"I'm very orthodox in some ways," Barbara remarked. "I've been brought up to suspect the least likely person. That's who it is in all the best murder mysteries. And Tredwell is certainly the least likely person."

"Except you, perhaps," Hastings suggested with a laugh.

"Oh, me!" Barbara smiled uncertainly as she rose and moved away from him. "How curious—" she murmured to herself.

"What's curious?" Hastings asked, rising to his feet.

"Something I've just thought of. Let's go out in the garden. I hate it in here." She moved towards the French windows.

"I'm afraid I have to stay here," Hastings told her.

"Why?"

"I mustn't leave this room."

"You know," Barbara observed, "you've

got a complex about this room. Do you remember last night? There we all were,
completely shattered by the disappearance of the formula, and in you strode, and
produced the most marvellous anticlimax
by saying in your best conversational manner, 'What a delightful room, Mr. Amory.'
It was so funny when the two of you
walked in. There was this extraordinary little man with you, no more than five feet
four, but with an air of immense dignity.
And you, being oh, so polite."

"Poirot is rather odd at first sight, I admit," Hastings agreed. "And he has all
kinds of little foibles. For instance, he has
an absolute passion for neatness of any
kind. If he sees an ornament set crook-
edly, or a speck of dust, or even a slight
disarray in someone's attire, it's absolute
torture to him."

"You make such a wonderful contrast to
each other," Barbara said, laughing.

"Poirot's methods of detection are very
much his own, you know," Hastings continued. "Order and method are his gods.
He has a great disdain for tangible evidence, things like footprints and cigarette
ash, you know what I mean. In fact he

maintains that, taken by themselves, they would never enable a detective to solve a problem. The true work, he says, is done from within. And then he taps that egg-shaped head of his, and remarks with great satisfaction, 'The little grey cells of the brain—always remember the little grey cells, *mon ami*.' "

"Oh, I think he's a poppet," Barbara declared. "But not as sweet as you, with your 'What a delightful room!' "

"But it *is* a delightful room," Hastings insisted, sounding rather nettled.

"Personally, I don't agree with you," said Barbara. She took his hand and tried to pull him towards the open French windows. "Anyway, you've had quite enough of it for now. Come along."

"You don't understand," Hastings declared, taking his hand away from her. "I promised Poirot."

Barbara spoke slowly. "You promised Monsieur Poirot that you would not leave this room? But why?"

"I can't tell you that."

"Oh!" Barbara was silent for a moment or two, and then her manner changed. She

moved behind Hastings and began to re-
cite, in an exaggerated dramatic voice,
'The boy stood on the burning deck—' "

"I beg your pardon?"

" 'Whence all but he had fled.' Well, my
pet?"

"I simply cannot understand you," Hastings declared in exasperation.

"Why should you understand me? Oh,
you really are a delight," declared Barbara, slipping her arm through his. "Come
and be vamped. Really, you know, I think
you're adorable."

"You're pulling my leg."

"Not at all," Barbara insisted. "I'm crazy
about you. You're positively pre-war."

She pulled him to the French windows,
and this time Hastings allowed himself to
yield to the pressure of her arm. "You really are an extraordinary person," he told
her. "You're quite different from any girl
I've ever met."

"I'm delighted to hear it. That's a very
good sign," said Barbara, as they now
stood, face to face, framed in the open
windows.

"A good sign?"

"Yes, it makes a girl feel hopeful."

Hastings blushed, and Barbara laughed light-heartedly as she dragged him out into the garden.

CHAPTER SIXTEEN

After Barbara's exit with Hastings into the garden, the library remained unoccupied for no longer than a moment or two. Then the door to the hall opened, and Miss Amory entered, carrying a small work-bag. She went over to the settee, put the bag down, knelt, and began to feel at the back of the seat. As she did so, Dr. Carelli entered by the other door, carrying a hat and a small suitcase. Seeing Miss Amory, Carelli stopped and murmured a word of apology at having intruded upon her.

Miss Amory rose from the settee, looking a trifle flustered. "I was searching for

a knitting needle," she explained unnec-
essarily, brandishing her discovery as she
spoke. "It had slipped down behind the
seat." Then, taking in the significance of
his suitcase, she asked, "Are you leaving
us, Dr. Carelli?"

Carelli put his hat and suitcase on a
chair. "I feel I can no longer trespass on
your hospitality," he announced.

Obviously delighted, Miss Amory was
polite enough to murmur, "Well, of course,
if you feel like that—" Then, remembering
the situation in which the occupants of the
house currently found themselves, she
added, "But I thought there were some
tiresome formalities—" Her voice trailed
off indecisively.

"Oh, that is all arranged," Carelli assured her.

"Well, if you feel you must go—"

"I do, indeed."

"Then I will order the car," Miss Amory
declared briskly, moving to the bell above
the fireplace.

"No, no," Carelli insisted. "That, too, is
all arranged."

"But you've even had to carry your suitcase down yourself. Really, the servants!

They're all demoralized, completely demoralized!" She returned to the settee and took her knitting from her bag. "They can't concentrate, Dr. Carelli. They cannot keep their heads. So curious, is it not?"

Looking distinctly on edge, Carelli replied offhandedly, "Very curious." He glanced at the telephone.

Miss Amory began to knit, keeping up a flow of aimless conversation as she did so. "I suppose you are catching the twelve-fifteen. You mustn't run it too fine. Not that I want to fuss, of course. I always say that fussing over—"

"Yes, indeed," Dr. Carelli interrupted peremptorily, "but there is plenty of time, I think. I—I wondered if I might use the telephone?"

Miss Amory looked up momentarily. "Oh, yes, of course," she said, as she continued to knit. It seemed not to have occurred to her that Dr. Carelli might have wanted to make his telephone call in private.

"Thank you," murmured Carelli, moving to the desk and making a pretence of looking up a number in the telephone directory. He glanced across impatiently at Miss

Amory. "I think your niece was looking for you," he remarked.

Miss Amory's only reaction to this information was to talk about her niece while continuing with her knitting undisturbed. "Dear Barbara!" she exclaimed. "Such a sweet creature. You know, she leads rather a sad life here, far too dull for a young girl. Well, well, things will be different now, I dare say." She dwelt pleasurably on this thought for a moment, before continuing, "Not that I haven't done all I could. But what a girl needs is a little gaiety. All the Beeswax in the world won't make up for that."

Dr. Carelli's face was a study in incomprehension, mixed with more than a little irritation. "Beeswax?" he felt obliged to ask.

"Yes, Beeswax—or is it Beemax? Vitamins, you know, or at least that's what it says on the tin. A and B and C and D. All of them, except the one that keeps you from having beriberi. And I really think there's no need for that, if one is living in England. It's not a disease one encounters here. It comes, I believe, from polishing the rice in native countries. So interesting.

I made Mr. Raynor take it—Beeswax, I mean—after breakfast every day. He was looking pale, poor young fellow. I tried to make Lucia take it, too, but she wouldn't." Miss Amory shook her head disapprovingly. "And to think, when I was a girl, I was strictly forbidden to eat caramels because of the Beeswax—I mean Beemax. Times change, you know. Times do change."

Though he attempted to disguise the fact, by now Dr. Carelli was positively fuming. "Yes, yes, Miss Amory," he replied as politely as he could manage. Moving towards her, he tried a somewhat more direct approach. "I think your niece is calling you."

"Calling me?"

"Yes. Do you not hear?"

Miss Amory listened. "No—no," she confessed. "How curious." She rolled up her knitting. "You must have keen ears, Dr. Carelli. Not that my hearing is bad. Indeed, I've been told that—"

She dropped her ball of wool, and Carelli picked it up for her. "Thank you so much," she said. "All the Amorys have keen hearing, you know." She rose from the settee. "My father kept his faculties in the most remarkable way. He could read without glasses when he was eighty." She dropped the ball of wool again, and again Carelli stooped to retrieve it for her.

"Oh, thank you so much," Miss Amory continued. "A remarkable man, Dr. Carelli. My father, I mean. Such a remarkable man. He always slept in a four-poster feather-bed; and the windows of his bedroom were never opened. The night air, he used to say, was most injurious. Unfortunately, when he had an attack of gout he was nursed by a young woman who insisted on the window being opened at the top, and my poor father died of it."

She dropped the ball of wool yet again. This time, after picking it up, Carelli planted it firmly in her hand and led her to the door. Miss Amory moved slowly, talking all the time. "I do not care at all for hospital nurses, Dr. Carelli," she informed him. "They gossip about their cases, they drink far too much tea, and they always upset the servants."

"Very true, dear lady, very true," Carelli agreed hastily, opening the door for her.

"Thank you so much," Miss Amory said

as he propelled her out of the room. Shutting the door after her, Carelli moved quickly to the desk and lifted the telephone receiver. After a pause, he spoke into it softly but urgently. "This is Market Cleve three-oh-four. I want London . . . Soho double-eight-five-three . . . no, five-three, that's right . . . Eh? . . . Will you call me? . . . Right."

He replaced the receiver and then stood biting his nails impatiently. After a moment he crossed to the door of the study, opened it, and entered the room. Hardly had he done so, when Edward Raynor came into the library from the hall. Glancing around the room, Raynor strolled casually to the fireplace. He touched the vase of spills on the mantelpiece, and as he did so, Carelli strolled into the room again from the study. As Carelli closed the study door, Raynor turned and saw him.

"I didn't know you were in here," said the secretary.

"I'm waiting for a phone call," Carelli explained.

"Oh!"

After a pause, Carelli spoke again. "When did the police inspector come?"

"About twenty minutes ago, I believe. Have you seen him?"

"Only in the distance," replied Carelli.

"He's a Scotland Yard man," Raynor informed him. "Apparently, he happened to be down in the neighbourhood clearing up some other case, so he was called in by the local police."

"That was a piece of luck, eh?" observed Carelli.

"Wasn't it?" The telephone rang, and Raynor moved towards it. Walking quickly ahead of him to the phone, Carelli said, "I think that will be my call." He looked at Raynor. "I wonder if you'd mind—"

"Certainly, my dear fellow," the secretary assured him. "I'll clear out."

Raynor left the room, and Carelli lifted the receiver. He spoke quietly. "Hello? . . . Is that Miguel? . . . Yes? . . . No, damn it, I haven't. It's been impossible . . . No, you don't understand, the old gentleman died last night . . . I'm leaving at once . . . Japp's here . . . Japp. You know, the Scotland Yard man . . . No, I've not met him yet . . . I hope so, too . . . At the usual place, nine-thirty tonight . . . Right."

Replacing the receiver, Carelli moved to

the recess, picked up his suitcase, put on his hat, and went towards the French windows. At that moment, Hercule Poirot entered from the garden, and he and Carelli collided. "I beg your pardon," said the Italian.

"Not at all," replied Poirot politely, continuing to block the way out.

"If you would allow me to pass—"

"Impossible," said Poirot mildly. "Quite impossible."

"I insist."

"I shouldn't," murmured Poirot with a friendly smile.

Suddenly, Carelli charged at Poirot. The little detective stepped briskly aside, tripping Carelli up neatly with an unexpected movement, and taking the Italian doctor's suitcase from him at the same time. At that moment, Japp slid into the room behind Poirot, and Carelli fell into the Inspector's arms.

"Hello, what's all this?" exclaimed Inspector Japp. "Why, bless me if it isn't Tonio!"

"Ah!" Poirot gave a little laugh as he moved away from them both. "I thought, my dear Japp, that you would probably be able to give a name to this gentleman."

"Oh, I know all about *him,*" Japp affirmed. "Tonio's quite a public character. Aren't you, Tonio? I'll bet you were surprised at Monsieur Poirot's move just then. What do you call that stuff, Poirot? Ju-jitsu or suchlike, isn't it? Poor old Tonio!"

As Poirot placed the Italian's suitcase on the table and opened it, Carelli growled at Japp, "You've got nothing against me. You can't hold me."

"I wonder," said the Inspector. "I'll bet we won't have far to look for the man who stole that formula, and did in the old gentleman." Turning to Poirot, he added, "That formula is absolutely bang in Tonio's line, and since we've found him trying to make a getaway, I shouldn't be surprised if he's got the goods on him this minute."

"I agree with you," declared Poirot.

Japp ran his hands over Carelli, while Poirot went through the suitcase.

"Well?" Japp asked Poirot.

"Nothing," the detective replied, closing the suitcase. "Nothing. I am disappointed."

"You think yourselves very clever, do

you not?" snarled Carelli. "But I could tell you—"

Poirot interrupted him, speaking quietly and significantly. "You could, perhaps, but it would be very unwise."

Startled, Carelli exclaimed, "What do you mean?"

"Monsieur Poirot's quite right," Japp declared. "You'd better keep your mouth shut." Moving to the hall door, he opened it and called, "Johnson!" The young constable put his head around the door. "Get the whole family together for me, will you?" Japp asked him. "I want them all here."

"Yes, sir," said Johnson as he left the room.

"I protest! I—" Carelli gasped. Suddenly, he grabbed his suitcase and made a dash towards the French windows. Japp rushed after him, grabbed him, and threw him onto the settee, taking the suitcase from him as he did so. "No one's hurt you yet, so don't squeal," Japp barked at the now thoroughly cowed Italian.

Poirot strolled towards the French windows. "Please don't go away now, Poirot," Japp called after him, putting Carelli's suitcase down by the coffee-table. "This should be very interesting."

"No, no, my dear Japp, I am not leaving," Poirot assured him. "I shall be right here. This family gathering, as you say, will be most interesting indeed."

CHAPTER SEVENTEEN

A few minutes later, when the Amory family began to assemble in the library, Carelli was still seated on the settee, looking rather sullen, while Poirot continued to hover by the French windows. Barbara Amory, with Hastings in tow, returned from the garden through the French windows, and Barbara moved to share the settee with Carelli, while Hastings went to stand by Poirot's side. Poirot whispered to his colleague, "It would be helpful, Hastings, if you would make a note—a mental note, you understand—of where they all choose to sit."

"Helpful? How?" asked Hastings.

"Psychologically, my friend" was Poirot's only reply.

When Lucia entered the room, Hastings watched her as she sat on a chair near the centre table. Richard arrived with his aunt, Miss Amory, who sat on the stool as Richard moved close to the table to keep a protective eye on his wife. Edward Raynor was the last to arrive, taking up a position behind the arm-chair. He was followed into the room by the constable, Johnson, who shut the door and stood close to it.

Richard Amory introduced Inspector Japp to those two members of the family whom Japp had not already met. "My aunt, Miss Amory," he announced, "and my cousin, Miss Barbara Amory."

Acknowledging the introduction, Barbara asked, "What's all the excitement, Inspector?"

Japp avoided her question. "Now, I think we're all here, are we not?" he remarked, moving to the fireplace.

Miss Amory looked bewildered and a little apprehensive. "I don't quite understand," she said to Richard. "What is this—this gentleman doing here?"

"I think perhaps I ought to tell you something," Richard answered her. "You see, Aunt Caroline—and all of you," he added, glancing around the room, "Dr. Graham has discovered that my father was—poisoned."

"What?" exclaimed Raynor sharply. Miss Amory gave a cry of horror.

"He was poisoned with hyoscine," Richard continued.

Raynor gave a start. "With hyoscine? Why, I saw—" He stopped dead, looking at Lucia.

Taking a step towards him, Inspector Japp asked, "What did you see, Mr. Raynor?"

The secretary looked embarrassed. "Nothing—at least—" he began uncertainly. His voice trailed off into silence.

"I'm sorry, Mr. Raynor," Japp insisted, "but I've got to have the truth. Come now, everyone realizes you're keeping something back."

"It's nothing, really," said the secretary. "I mean, there's obviously some quite reasonable explanation."

"Explanation for what, Mr. Raynor?" asked Japp.

Raynor still hesitated.

"Well?" Japp prompted him.

"It was only that—" Raynor paused again, and then made up his mind to continue. "It was only that I saw Mrs. Amory emptying out some of those little tablets into her hand."

"When was this?" Japp asked him.

"Last night. I was coming out of Sir Claud's study. The others were busy with the gramophone. They were all clustered around it. I noticed her pick up a tube of tablets—I thought it was the hyoscine—and pour most of them out into the palm of her hand. Then Sir Claud called me back into the study for something."

"Why didn't you mention this before?" asked Japp.

Lucia began to speak, but the Inspector silenced her. "One minute, please, Mrs. Amory," he insisted. "I'd like to hear from Mr. Raynor first."

"I never thought of it again," Raynor told him. "It was only when Mr. Amory said just now that Sir Claud had been poisoned with hyoscine that it came back to me. Of course, I realize it's perfectly all right. It was just the coincidence that startled me.

The tablets might not have been hyoscine at all. It could have been one of the other tubes that she was handling."

Japp now turned to Lucia. "Well, ma'am," he asked, "what have you got to say about it?"

Lucia seemed quite composed as she answered, "I wanted something to make me sleep."

Addressing Raynor again, Japp asked, "You say she pretty well emptied the tube?"

"It seemed so to me," said Raynor.

Japp turned again to Lucia. "You wouldn't have needed so many tablets to make you sleep. One or two would have been sufficient. What did you do with the rest?"

Lucia thought for a moment before replying, "I can't remember." She was about to continue, when Carelli rose to his feet and burst out venomously, "You see, Inspector? There's your murderess."

Barbara rose quickly from the settee and moved away from Carelli, while Hastings hurried to her side. The Italian continued, "You shall have the truth, Inspector. I came down here especially to see that woman. She had sent for me. She said she would get Sir Claud's formula, and she offered to sell it to me. I'll admit that I've dealt with such things in the past."

"That's not much of an admission," Japp advised him, moving between Carelli and Lucia. "We know as much already." He turned to Lucia. "What have you to say to all this, ma'am?"

Lucia rose, her face drained of colour, and Richard went to her. "I'm not going to allow—" he began, when Japp stopped him.

"If you please, sir."

Carelli spoke again. "Just look at that woman! None of you know who she is. But I do! She's the daughter of Selma Goetz. The daughter of one of the most infamous women the world has ever known."

"It's not true, Richard," Lucia cried. "It's not true! Don't listen to him—"

"I'll break every bone in your body!" Richard Amory growled at Carelli.

Japp took a pace towards Richard. "Keep calm, sir, do keep calm, please," he admonished. "We've got to get to the bottom of this." Japp turned to Lucia. "Now then, Mrs. Amory."

There was a pause. Lucia tried to speak. "I—I—" she began. She looked at her husband and then at Poirot, holding out her hand helplessly to the detective.

"Have courage, madame," Poirot advised her. "Trust in me. Tell them. Tell them the truth. We have come to the point where lies will serve no longer. The truth will have to come out."

Lucia looked pleadingly at Poirot, but he merely repeated, "Have courage, madame. *Si, si*. Be brave and speak." He returned to his position by the French windows.

After a long pause, Lucia began to speak, her voice low and stifled. "It is true that I am Selma Goetz's daughter. It is *not* true that I asked that man to come here, or that I offered to sell him Sir Claud's formula. He came here to blackmail me!"

"Blackmail!" gasped Richard, moving to her.

Lucia turned to Richard. There was an urgency in her tone as she spoke. "He threatened to tell you about my mother unless I got the formula for him, but I didn't do it. I think he must have stolen it. He had the chance. He was alone in there—in the study. And I see now that he wanted me to take the hyoscine and kill myself, so that everyone would think that it was I who had stolen the formula. He almost hypnotized me into—" She broke down and sobbed on Richard's shoulder.

With a cry of "Lucia, my darling!" Richard embraced her. Then, passing his wife over to Miss Amory, who had risen and who now embraced the distressed young woman consolingly, Richard addressed Japp. "Inspector, I want to speak to you alone."

Japp looked at Richard Amory for a moment and then gave a brief nod to Johnson. "Very well," he agreed, as the constable opened the door for Miss Amory and Lucia. Barbara and Hastings took the opportunity of returning to the garden through the French windows, while Edward Raynor, as he left, murmured to Richard, "I'm sorry, Mr. Amory, very sorry."

As Carelli picked up his suitcase and followed Raynor out, Japp instructed his constable, "Keep your eye on Mrs. Amory—and also on Dr. Carelli." Carelli turned at the door, and Japp continued, to the constable, "There's to be no funny business from anyone, you understand?"

"I understand, sir," replied Johnson as he followed Carelli out of the room.

"I'm sorry, Mr. Amory," said Japp to Richard Amory, "but after what Mr. Raynor has told us, I'm bound to take every precaution. And I want Monsieur Poirot to remain here, as a witness to whatever you tell me."

Richard approached Japp with the air of a man who has come to a momentous decision. Taking a deep breath, he spoke with determination. "Inspector!"

"Well, sir, what is it?" asked Japp.

Very deliberately and slowly, Richard replied, "I think it's time I confessed. I killed my father."

Japp smiled. "I'm afraid that won't wash, sir."

Richard looked astonished. "What do you mean?"

"No, sir," Japp continued. "Or, to put it differently, that cat won't jump. You're very set on your good lady, I realize. Newly married and all that. But, to speak plainly to you, it's no manner of use putting your neck in a halter for the sake of a bad woman. Though she's a good-looker, and no mistake, I'll admit."

"Inspector Japp!" exclaimed Richard angrily.

"There's no point in getting upset with me, sir," Japp continued imperturbably. "I've told you the plain truth without beating about the bush, and I've no doubt that Monsieur Poirot here will tell you the same. I'm sorry, sir, but duty is duty, and murder is murder. That's all there is to it." Japp nodded decisively and left the room.

Turning to Poirot, who had been observing the scene from the settee, Richard asked coldly, "Well, *are* you going to tell me the same, Monsieur Poirot?"

Rising, Poirot took a cigarette-case from his pocket and extracted a cigarette. Instead of answering Richard's question, he posed one of his own. "Monsieur Amory, when did you first suspect your wife?" he asked.

"I never—" Richard began, but Poirot interrupted him, picking up a box of matches from the table as he spoke.

"Please, I beg of you, Monsieur Amory, nothing but the truth! You did suspect her, I know it. You suspected her before I arrived. That is why you were so anxious to get me away from this house. Do not deny it. It is impossible to deceive Hercule Poirot." He lit his cigarette, replaced the box of matches on the table, and smiled up at the much taller man, who towered over him. They made a ridiculous contrast.

"You are mistaken," Richard told Poirot stiffly. "Utterly mistaken. How could I suspect Lucia?"

"And yet, of course, there is an equally good case to be made against you," Poirot continued reflectively, as he resumed his seat. "You handled the drugs, you handled the coffee, you were short of money and desperate to acquire some. Oh, yes, anyone might be excused for suspecting you."

"Inspector Japp doesn't seem to agree with you," Richard observed.

"Ah, Japp! He has the common sense," Poirot smiled. "He is not a woman in love."

"A woman in love?" Richard sounded puzzled.

"Let me give you a lesson in psychology, monsieur," Poirot offered. "When I first arrived, your wife came up to me and begged me to stay here and discover the murderer. Would a guilty woman have done that?"

"You mean—" Richard began quickly.

"I mean," Poirot interrupted him, "that before the sun sets tonight, you will be asking her pardon upon your knees."

"What are you saying?"

"I am saying too much, perhaps," Poirot admitted, rising. "Now, monsieur, place yourself in my hands. In the hands of Hercule Poirot."

"You can save her?" Richard asked with desperation in his voice.

Poirot regarded him solemnly. "I have pledged my word—although, when I did so, I did not realize how difficult it was going to be. You see, the time it is very short, and something must be done quickly. You must promise me that you will do exactly as I tell you, without asking questions or making difficulties. Do you promise me that?"

"Very well," replied Richard rather unwillingly.

"That is good. And now, listen to me. What I suggest is neither difficult nor impossible. It is, in fact, the common sense. This house will shortly be given over to the police. They will swarm all over it. They will make their investigations everywhere. For yourself and your family it could be very unpleasant. I suggest that you leave."

"Give the house over to the police?" Richard asked, incredulous.

"That is my suggestion," Poirot repeated. "Of course, you will have to remain in the neighbourhood. But they say the local hotel is fairly comfortable. Engage rooms there. Then you will be close at hand when the police wish to question you all."

"But when do you suggest that this should take place?"

Poirot beamed at him. "My idea was—immediately."

"Surely it will all look very odd?"

"Not at all, not at all," the little detective assured Richard, smiling again. "It will appear to be a move of the utmost—how do you say?—the utmost sensitivity. The associations here are hateful to you—you cannot bear to remain another hour. I assure you, it will sound very well."

"But how about the Inspector?"

"I myself will fix it up with Inspector Japp."

"I still can't see what good this is going to achieve," Richard persisted.

"No, of course you do not see." Poirot sounded more than a trifle smug. He shrugged his shoulders. "It is not necessary that you should see. But I see. I, Hercule Poirot. That is enough." He took Richard by the shoulders. "Go, and make the arrangements. Or, if you cannot give your mind to it, let Raynor make them for you. Go! Go!" He almost pushed Richard to the door.

With a final anxious look back at Poirot, Richard left the room. "Oh, these English! How obstinate," muttered Poirot. He moved to the French windows and called, "Mademoiselle Barbara!"

CHAPTER EIGHTEEN

In answer to Poirot's call, Barbara Amory appeared outside the French windows. "What is it? Has something else happened?" she asked.

Poirot gave her his most winning smile. "Ah, mademoiselle," he said. "I wonder if you might be able to spare my colleague Hastings for just a little minute or two, perhaps?"

Barbara's reply was accompanied by a skittish glance. "So! You want to take my little pet away from me, do you?"

"Just for a very short time, mademoiselle, I promise you."

"Then you shall, Monsieur Poirot." Turning back into the garden, Barbara called, "My pet, you're wanted."

"I thank you," Poirot smiled again with a polite bow. Barbara returned to the garden, and a few moments later Hastings entered the library through the French windows, looking somewhat ashamed.

"And what have you to say for yourself?" Poirot asked in a tone of mock annoyance.

Hastings attempted an apologetic smile. "It is all very well to put on the grin of the sheep," Poirot admonished him. "I leave you here on guard, and the next thing I know you are promenading yourself with that very charming young lady in the garden. You are generally the most reliable of men, *mon cher,* but as soon as a pretty young woman appears upon the scene, your judgement flies out of the window. *Zut alors!*"

Hastings's sheepish grin faded, to be replaced by a blush of embarrassment. "I say, I'm awfully sorry, Poirot," he exclaimed. "I just stepped outside for a second, and then I saw you through the window, coming into the room, so I thought it didn't matter."

"You mean you thought it better not to return to face me," declared Poirot. "Well, my dear Hastings, you may have done the most irreparable damage. I found Carelli in here. The good Lord alone knows what he was doing, or what evidence he was tampering with."

"I say, Poirot, I really am sorry," Hastings apologized again. "I'm most awfully sorry."

"If you have not done the damage irreparable, it is more by good luck than for any other reason. But now, *mon ami,* the moment has come when we must employ our little grey cells." Pretending to smack Hastings on the cheek, Poirot in fact gave his colleague an affectionate pat.

"Ah, good! Let's get to work," Hastings exclaimed.

"No, it is not good, my friend," Poirot told him. "It is bad. It is obscure." His face wore a troubled look as he continued, "It is dark, as dark as it was last night." He thought for a moment, and then added, "But—yes—I think there is perhaps an idea. The germ of an idea. Yes, we will start there!"

Looking completely mystified, Hastings asked, "What on earth are you talking about?"

The tone of Poirot's voice changed. He spoke gravely and thoughtfully. "Why did Sir Claud die, Hastings? Answer me that. Why did Sir Claud die?"

Hastings stared at him. "But we know that," he exclaimed.

"Do we?" asked Poirot. "Are you so very sure?"

"Er—yes," Hastings responded, though somewhat uncertainly. "He died—he died because he was poisoned."

Poirot made an impatient gesture. "Yes, but *why* was he poisoned?"

Hastings thought carefully before replying. Then, "Surely it must have been because the thief suspected—" he began.

Poirot slowly shook his head as Hastings continued, "because the thief suspected— that he had been discovered—" He broke off again as he observed Poirot continuing to shake his head.

"Suppose, Hastings—" Poirot murmured, "just suppose that the thief did not suspect?"

"I don't quite see," Hastings confessed.

Poirot moved away, and then turned back with his arm raised in a gesture that seemed intended to hold his friend's attention. He paused and cleared his throat. "Let me recount to you, Hastings," he declared, "the sequence of events as they might have gone, or rather as I think they were meant to go."

Hastings sat in a chair by the table as Poirot continued.

"Sir Claud dies in his chair one night." Poirot moved to the arm-chair, sat, and paused for a moment before repeating thoughtfully, "Yes, Sir Claud dies in his chair. There are no suspicious circumstances attending that death. In all probability it will be put down to heart failure. It will be some days before his private papers are examined. His will is the only document that will be searched for. After the funeral, in due course, it will be discovered that his notes on the new explosive are incomplete. It may never be known that the exact formula existed. You see what that gives to our thief, Hastings?"

"Yes."

"What?" asked Poirot.

Hastings looked puzzled. "What?" he repeated.

"Security. That is what it gives the thief. He can dispose of his booty quite safely, whenever he wishes to. There is no pressure upon him. Even if the existence of the formula is known, he will have had plenty of time to cover his tracks."

"Well, it's an idea—yes, I suppose so," Hastings commented in a dubious tone.

"But naturally it is an idea!" Poirot cried. "Am I not Hercule Poirot? But see now where this idea leads us. It tells us that the murder of Sir Claud was not a chance manoeuvre executed on the spur of the moment. It was planned beforehand. Beforehand. You see now where we are?"

"No," Hastings admitted with an engaging candour. "You know very well I never see these things. I know that we're in the library of Sir Claud's house, and that's all."

"Yes, my friend, you are right," Poirot told him. "We are in the library of Sir Claud Amory's house. It is not morning but evening. The lights have just gone out. The thief's plans have gone awry."

Poirot sat very upright and wagged his forefinger emphatically to emphasize his points. "Sir Claud, who, in the normal course of things, would not have gone to that safe until the following day, has discovered his loss by a mere chance. And, as the old gentleman himself said, the thief is caught like a rat in a trap. Yes, but the thief, who is also the murderer, knows something, too, that Sir Claud does not. The thief knows that in a very few minutes Sir Claud will be silenced for ever. He—or she—has one problem that has to be solved, and one only—to hide the paper safely during those few moments of darkness. Shut your eyes, Hastings, as I shut mine. The lights have gone out, and we can see nothing. But we can hear. Repeat to me, Hastings, as accurately as you can, the words of Miss Amory when she described this scene for us."

Hastings shut his eyes. Then he began to speak, slowly, with an effort of memory and several pauses. "Gasps," he uttered.

Poirot nodded. "A lot of little gasps," Hastings went on, and Poirot nodded again.

Hastings concentrated for a time, and

then continued, "The noise of a chair fall-ing—a metallic clink—that must have been the key, I imagine."

"Quite right," said Poirot. "The key. Continue."

"A scream. That was Lucia screaming. She called out to Sir Claud—Then the knocking came at the door—Oh! Wait a moment—right at the beginning, the noise of tearing silk." Hastings opened his eyes.

"Yes, tearing silk," Poirot exclaimed. He rose, moved to the desk, and then crossed to the fireplace. "It is all there, Hastings, in those few moments of darkness. All there. And yet our ears tell us—nothing." He stopped at the mantelpiece and mechani-cally straightened the vase of spills.

"Oh, do stop straightening those damned things, Poirot," Hastings complained. "You're always at it."

His attention arrested, Poirot removed his hand from the vase. "What is that you say?" he asked. "Yes, it is true." He stared at the vase of spills. "I remember straight-ening them but a little hour ago. And now—it is necessary that I straighten them again." He spoke excitedly. "Why, Has-tings—why is that?"

"Because they're crooked, I suppose," Hastings replied in a bored tone. "It's just your little mania for neatness."

"Tearing silk!" exclaimed Poirot. "No, Hastings! The sound is the same." He stared at the paper spills, and snatched up the vase that contained them. "Tearing paper," he continued as he moved away from the mantelpiece.

His excitement communicated itself to his friend. "What is it?" Hastings asked, springing up and moving to him.

Poirot stood, tumbling out the spills onto the settee, and examining them. Every now and then he handed one to Hastings, muttering, "Here is one. Ah, another, and yet another."

Hastings unfolded the spills and scrutinized them. "C19 N23—" he began to read aloud from one of them.

"Yes, yes!" exclaimed Poirot. "It is the formula!"

"I say, that's wonderful!"

"Quick! Fold them up again!" Poirot ordered, and Hastings began to do so. "Oh, you are so slow!" Poirot admonished him. "Quick! Quick!" Snatching the spills from Hastings, he put them back into the vase and hastened to return it to the mantelpiece.

Looking dumbfounded, Hastings joined him there.

Poirot beamed. "It intrigues you what I do there, yes? Tell me, Hastings, what is it that I have here in this vase?"

"Why, spills, of course," Hastings replied in a tone of tremendous irony.

"No, *mon ami*, it is cheese."

"Cheese?"

"Precisely, my friend, cheese."

"I say, Poirot," Hastings inquired sarcastically, "you're all right, aren't you? I mean, you haven't got a headache or anything?"

Poirot's reply ignored his friend's frivolous question. "For what do you use cheese, Hastings? I will tell you, *mon ami*. You use it to bait a mousetrap. We wait now for one thing only—the mouse."

"And the mouse—"

"The mouse will come, my friend," Poirot assured Hastings. "Rest assured of that. I have sent him a message. He will not fail to respond."

Before Hastings had time to react to Poirot's cryptic announcement, the door opened and Edward Raynor entered the room. "Oh, you're here, Monsieur Poirot," the secretary observed. "And Captain Hastings also. Inspector Japp would like to speak to you both upstairs."

CHAPTER NINETEEN

"We will come at once," Poirot replied. Followed by Hastings, he walked to the door, as Raynor entered the library and crossed to the fireplace. At the door, Poirot suddenly wheeled round to look at the secretary. "By the way, Mr. Raynor," the detective asked, as he moved back to the centre of the room, "do you by any chance know whether Dr. Carelli was here in the library at all this morning?"

"Yes, he was," Raynor told the detective. "I found him here."

"Ah!" Poirot seemed pleased at this. "And what was he doing?"

"He was telephoning, I believe."

"Was he telephoning when you came in?"

"No, he was just coming back into the room. He had been in Sir Claud's study."

Poirot considered this for a moment, and then asked Raynor, "Where exactly were you then? Can you remember?"

Still standing by the fireplace, Raynor replied, "Oh, somewhere about here, I think."

"Did you hear any of Dr. Carelli's conversation on the phone?"

"No," said the secretary. "He made it perfectly clear that he wanted to be alone, so I cleared out."

"I see." Poirot hesitated, and then took a notebook and pencil from his pocket. Writing a few words on a page, he tore it out. "Hastings!" he called.

Hastings, who had been hovering by the door, came to him, and Poirot gave his friend the folded page. "Would you be so kind as to take that up to Inspector Japp?"

Raynor watched Hastings leave the room on his errand, and then asked, "What was that all about?"

Putting the notebook and pencil back in

his pocket, Poirot replied, "I told Japp that I would be with him in a few minutes, and that I might be able to tell him the name of the murderer."

"Really? You know who it is?" asked Raynor in a state of some excitement.

There was a momentary pause. Hercule Poirot seemed to hold the secretary under the spell of his personality. Raynor watched the detective, fascinated, as he began slowly to speak. "Yes, I think I know who the murderer is—at last," Poirot announced. "I am reminded of another case, not so long ago. Never shall I forget the killing of Lord Edgware. I was nearly defeated—yes, I, Hercule Poirot!—by the extremely simple cunning of a vacant brain. You see, Monsieur Raynor, the very simple-minded have often the genius to commit an uncomplicated crime and then leave it alone. Let us hope that the murderer of Sir Claud, on the other hand, is intelligent and superior and thoroughly pleased with himself and unable to resist— how do you say?—painting the lily." Poirot's eyes lit up in vivid animation.

"I'm not sure that I understand you,"

said Raynor. "Do you mean that it's *not* Mrs. Amory?"

"No, it is not Mrs. Amory," Poirot told him. "That is why I wrote my little note. That poor lady has suffered enough. She must be spared any further questioning."

Raynor looked thoughtful, and then exclaimed, "Then I'll bet it's Carelli. Yes?"

Poirot wagged a finger at him playfully. "Monsieur Raynor, you must permit me to keep my little secrets until the last moment." Taking out a handkerchief, he mopped his brow. "*Mon Dieu,* how hot it is today!" he complained.

"Would you like a drink?" asked Raynor. "I'm forgetting my manners. I should have offered you one earlier."

Poirot beamed. "You are very kind. I will have a whisky, please, if I may."

"Certainly. Just a moment." Raynor left the room, while Poirot wandered across to the French windows and looked out into the garden for a moment. Then, moving to the settee, he shook the cushions, before drifting across to the mantelpiece to examine the ornaments. In a few moments Raynor returned with two whiskies and sodas on a tray. He watched as Poirot lifted a hand to an ornament on the mantelpiece.

"This is a valuable antique, I fancy," Poirot remarked, picking up a jug.

"Is it?" was Raynor's uninterested comment. "I don't know much about that kind of thing. Come and have a drink," he suggested as he set his tray down on the coffee-table.

"Thank you," murmured Poirot, joining him there.

"Well, here's luck," said Raynor, taking a glass and drinking.

With a bow, Poirot raised the other glass to his lips. "To you, my friend. And now let me tell you of my suspicions. I first realized that—"

He broke off suddenly, jerking his head over his shoulder as though some sound had caught his ear. Looking first at the door and then at Raynor, he put his finger to his lips, indicating that he thought someone might be eavesdropping.

Raynor nodded in comprehension. The two men crept stealthily up to the door, and Poirot gestured to the secretary to remain in the room. Poirot opened the door sharply and bounced outside, but returned immediately looking extremely crestfallen. "Surprising," he admitted to Raynor. "I could have sworn I heard something. Ah well, I made a mistake. It does not happen very often. *A votre santé,* my friend." He drained the contents of his glass.

"Ah!" exclaimed Raynor, as he also drank.

"I beg your pardon?" asked Poirot.

"Nothing. A load off my mind, that is all."

Poirot moved to the table and put his glass down. "Do you know, Monsieur Raynor," he confided, "to be absolutely honest with you, I have never become quite used to your English national drink, the whisky. The taste, it pleases me not. It is bitter." He moved to the arm-chair and sat.

"Really? I'm so sorry. Mine didn't taste at all bitter." Raynor put his glass down on the coffee-table, and continued, "I think you were about to tell me something just now, were you not?"

Poirot looked surprised. "Was I? What can it have been? Can I have forgotten already? I think that perhaps I wanted to explain to you how I proceed in an investigation. *Voyons!* One fact leads to another, so we continue. Does the next one fit in with that? *A merveille!* Good! We can proceed. This next little fact—no! Ah, that is curious! There is something missing—a link in the chain that is not there. We examine. We search. And that little curious fact, that perhaps paltry little detail that will not tally, we put it here!" Poirot made an extravagant gesture with his hand. "It is significant! It is tremendous!"

"Y-es, I see," Raynor murmured dubiously.

Poirot shook his forefinger so fiercely in Raynor's face that the secretary almost quailed before it. "Ah, beware! Peril to the detective who says, 'It is so small, it does not matter. It will not agree. I will forget it.' That way lies confusion! Everything matters." Poirot suddenly stopped and tapped his head. "Ah! Now I remember what I wanted to talk to you about. It was one of those small, unimportant little facts. I wanted to talk to you, Monsieur Raynor, about dust."

Raynor smiled politely. "Dust?"

"Precisely. Dust," Poirot repeated. "My friend Hastings, he reminded me just now that I am a detective and not a housemaid. He thought himself very clever to make such a remark, but I am not so sure. The housemaid and the detective, after all, have something in common. The housemaid, what does she do? She explores all the dark corners with her broom. She brings into the light of day all the hidden things that have rolled conveniently out of sight. Does not the detective do much the same?"

Raynor looked bored, but murmured, "Very interesting, Monsieur Poirot." He moved to the chair by the table and sat, before asking, "But—is that all you were intending to say?"

"No, not quite," replied Poirot. He leaned forward. "You did not throw dust in my eyes, Monsieur Raynor, because there was no dust. Do you understand?"

The secretary stared at him intently. "No, I'm afraid I don't."

"There was no dust on that box of drugs. Mademoiselle Barbara commented on the fact. But there should have been dust. That shelf on which it stands"—and Poirot gestured towards it as he spoke— "is thick with dust. It was then that I knew—"

"Knew what?"

"I knew," Poirot continued, "that some-one had taken that box down recently. That the person who poisoned Sir Claud Amory would not need to go near the box last night, since he had on some earlier occasion helped himself to all the poison he needed, choosing a time when he knew he would not be disturbed. You did not go near the box of drugs last night, because you had already taken from it the hyoscine you needed. But you did handle the coffee, Monsieur Raynor."

Raynor smiled patiently. "Dear me! Do you accuse me of murdering Sir Claud?"

"Do you deny it?" asked Poirot.

Raynor paused before replying. When he spoke again, a harsher tone had entered his voice. "Oh, no," he declared, "I don't deny it. Why should I? I'm really rather proud of the whole thing. It ought to have gone off without a hitch. It was sheer bad luck that made Sir Claud open the safe again last night. He's never done such a thing before."

Poirot sounded rather drowsy as he asked, "Why are you telling me all this?"

"Why not? You're so sympathetic. It's a pleasure to talk to you." Raynor laughed, and continued. "Yes, things very nearly went wrong. But that's what I really pride myself on, turning a failure into a success." A triumphant expression appeared on his face. "To devise a hiding place on the spur of the moment was really rather creditable. Would you like me to tell you where the formula is now?"

His drowsiness now accentuated, Poirot seemed to find difficulty in speaking clearly. "I—I do not understand you," he whispered.

"You made one little mistake, Monsieur Poirot," Raynor told him with a sneer. "You underestimated my intelligence. I wasn't really taken in just now by your ingenious red herring about poor old Carelli. A man with your brains couldn't seriously have believed that Carelli—why, it won't bear thinking about. You see, I'm playing for big stakes. That piece of paper, delivered in the right quarters, means fifty thousand pounds to me." He leaned back. "Just think what a man of my ability can do with fifty thousand pounds."

In a voice of increasing drowsiness, Poirot managed to reply, "I—I do not—like to think of it."

"Well, perhaps not. I appreciate that," Raynor conceded. "One has to allow for a different point of view."

Poirot leaned forward, and appeared to be making an effort to pull himself together. "And it will not be so," he exclaimed. I will denounce you. I, Hercule Poirot—" He broke off suddenly.

"Hercule Poirot will do nothing," declared Raynor, as the detective sank back in his seat. With a laugh which was close to a sneer, the secretary continued, "You never guessed, did you, even when you said that the whisky was bitter? You see, my dear Monsieur Poirot, I took not just one but several tubes of hyoscine from that box. If anything, you have had slightly more than I gave Sir Claud."

"Ah, *mon Dieu*," Poirot gasped, struggling to rise. In a weak voice he tried to call, "Hastings! Has——" His voice faded away, and he sank back into his chair. His eyelids closed.

Raynor got to his feet, pushed his chair aside, and moved to stand over Poirot. "Try to keep awake, Monsieur Poirot," he said. "Surely you'd like to see where the formula was hidden, wouldn't you?"

He waited for a moment, but Poirot's eyes remained closed. "A swift, dreamless sleep, and no awakening, as our dear friend Carelli puts it," Raynor commented drily as he went to the mantelpiece, took the spills, folded them, and put them in his pocket. He moved towards the French windows, pausing only to call over his shoulder, "Goodbye, my dear Monsieur Poirot."

He was about to step out into the garden when he was halted by the sound of Poirot's voice, speaking cheerfully and naturally. "Would you not like the envelope as well?"

Raynor spun around, and at the same moment Inspector Japp entered the library from the garden. Moving back a few steps, Raynor paused irresolutely, and then decided to bolt. He rushed to the French windows, only to be seized by Japp and by Constable Johnson, who also suddenly appeared from the garden.

Poirot rose from his chair, stretching himself. "Well, my dear Japp," he asked. "Did you get it all?"

Dragging Raynor back to the centre of the room with the aid of his constable,

Japp replied, "Every word, thanks to your note, Poirot. You can hear everything perfectly from the terrace there, just outside the window. Now, let's go over him and see what we can find." He pulled the spills from Raynor's pocket and threw them onto the coffee-table. He next pulled out a small tube. "Aha! Hyoscine! Empty."

"Ah, Hastings," Poirot greeted his friend, as he entered from the hall carrying a glass of whisky and soda, which he handed to the detective.

"You see?" Poirot addressed Raynor in his kindliest manner. "I refused to play in your comedy. Instead, I made you play in mine. In my note, I gave instructions to Japp and also to Hastings. Then I make things easy for you by complaining of the heat. I know you will suggest a drink. It is, after all, the opening that you need. After that, it is all so straightforward. When I go to the door, the good Hastings, he is ready outside with another whisky and soda. I change glasses and I am back again. And so—on with the comedy."

Poirot gave the glass back to Hastings. "Myself, I think I play my part rather well," he declared.

There was a pause while Poirot and Raynor surveyed each other. Then Raynor spoke. "I've been afraid of you ever since you came into this house. My scheme could have worked. I could have set myself up for life with the fifty thousand pounds—perhaps even more—that I would have got for that wretched formula. But, from the moment you arrived, I stopped feeling absolutely confident that I'd get away with killing that pompous old fool and stealing his precious scrap of paper."

"I have observed already that you are intelligent," Poirot replied. He sat again in the arm-chair, looking distinctly pleased with himself, as Japp began to speak rapidly.

"Edward Raynor, I arrest you for the wilful murder of Sir Claud Amory, and I warn you that anything you say may be used in evidence." Japp made a gesture to the constable to take Raynor away.

CHAPTER TWENTY

As Raynor made his exit in the custody of Constable Johnson, the two men passed Miss Amory, who was entering the library at the same moment. She looked back at them anxiously, and then hastened to Poirot. "Monsieur Poirot," she gasped as Poirot rose to greet her, "is this true? Was it Mr. Raynor who murdered my poor brother?"

"I am afraid so, mademoiselle," said Poirot.

Miss Amory looked dumbfounded. "Oh! Oh!" she exclaimed. "I can't believe it! What wickedness! We've always treated him like one of the family. And the Beeswax and everything—" She turned abruptly, and was about to leave when Richard entered and held the door open for her. As she almost ran from the room, her niece Barbara entered from the garden.

"This is simply too shattering for words," Barbara exclaimed. "Edward Raynor, of all people. Who would have believed it? Somebody has been frightfully clever to have found out. I wonder who!"

She looked meaningfully at Poirot who, however, gave a bow in the direction of the police inspector as he murmured, "It was Inspector Japp who solved the case, mademoiselle."

Japp beamed. "I will say for you, Monsieur Poirot, you're the goods. And a gentleman as well." With a nod to the assembled company, Japp made a brisk exit, snatching the whisky glass from a bemused Hastings, with the words, "I'll take charge of the evidence, if you please, Captain Hastings!"

"Yes, but was it really Inspector Japp who found out who killed Uncle Claud? Or," Barbara asked Poirot coyly as she approached him, "was it you, Monsieur Hercule Poirot?"

Poirot moved to Hastings, putting an arm around his old friend. "Mademoiselle," he informed Barbara, "the real credit belongs to Hastings here. He made a remark of surpassing brilliance which put me on the right track. Take him into the garden and make him tell you about it."

He pushed Hastings towards Barbara and shepherded them both towards the French windows. "Ah, my pet," Barbara sighed comically to Hastings as they went out into the garden.

Richard Amory was about to address Poirot, when the door to the hall opened and Lucia entered. Giving a start when she saw her husband, Lucia murmured uncertainly, "Richard—"

Richard turned to look at her. "Lucia!"

Lucia moved a few steps into the room. "I—" she began, and then broke off.

Richard approached her, and then stopped. "You—"

They both looked extremely nervous and ill at ease with each other. Then Lucia suddenly caught sight of Poirot and went to him with outstretched hands. "Monsieur Poirot! How can we ever thank you?"

Poirot took both her hands in his. "So, madame, your troubles are over!" he announced.

"A murderer has been caught. But my troubles, are they really over?" Lucia asked wistfully.

"It is true that you do not look quite happy yet, my child," Poirot observed.

"Shall I ever be happy again, I wonder?"

"I think so," said Poirot with a twinkle in his eye. "Trust in your old Poirot." Guiding Lucia to the chair by the table in the centre of the room, he picked up the spills from the coffee-table, went across to Richard, and handed them to him. "Monsieur," he declared, "I have pleasure in restoring to you Sir Claud's formula! It can be pieced together—what is the expression you use?—it will be as good as new."

"My God, the formula!" Richard exclaimed. "I'd almost forgotten it. I can hardly bear to look at it again. Think what it has done to us all. It's cost my father his life, and it's all but ruined the lives of all of us as well."

"What are you going to do with it, Richard?" Lucia asked him.

"I don't know. What would you do with it?"

Rising and moving to him, Lucia whispered, "Would you let me?"

"It's yours," her husband told her, handing her the spills. "Do as you like with the wretched thing."

"Thank you, Richard," murmured Lucia. She went to the fireplace, took a match from the box on the mantelpiece, and set fire to the spills, dropping the pieces one by one into the fireplace. "There is so much suffering already in the world. I cannot bear to think of any more."

"Madame," said Poirot, "I admire the manner in which you burn many thousands of pounds with as little emotion as though they were just a few pence."

"They are nothing but ashes," Lucia sighed. "Like my life."

Poirot gave a snort. *"Oh, là, là!* Let us all order our coffins," he remarked in a tone of mock gloom. "No! Me, I like to be happy, to rejoice, to dance, to sing. See you, my children," he continued, turning to address Richard as well, "I am about to take a liberty with you both. Madame looks down her nose and thinks, 'I have deceived my husband.' Monsieur looks down his nose and thinks, 'I have suspected my wife.' And yet what you really want, both of you, is to be in each other's arms, is it not?"

Lucia took a step towards her husband. "Richard—" she began in a low voice.

"Madame," Poirot interrupted her, "I fear that Sir Claud may have suspected you of planning to steal his formula because, a few weeks ago, someone—no doubt an ex-colleague of Carelli, for people of that kind are continually falling out with one another—someone, I say, sent Sir Claud an anonymous letter about your mother. But, do you know, my foolish child, that your husband tried to accuse himself to Inspector Japp—that he actually confessed to the murder of Sir Claud—in order to save you?"

Lucia gave a little cry, and looked adoringly at Richard.

"And you, monsieur," Poirot continued. "Figure to yourself that, not more than half an hour ago, your wife was shouting in my ear that she had killed your father, all because she feared that you might have done so."

"Lucia," Richard murmured tenderly, going to her.

"Being English," Poirot remarked as he moved away from them, "you will not embrace in my presence, I suppose?"

Lucia went to him and took his hand. "Monsieur Poirot, I do not think I shall ever forget you—ever."

"Neither shall I forget you, madame," Poirot declared gallantly as he kissed her hand.

"Poirot," Richard Amory declared, "I don't know what to say, except that you've saved my life and my marriage: I can't express what I feel—"

"Do not derange yourself, my friend," replied Poirot. "I am happy to have been of service to you."

Lucia and Richard went out into the garden together, looking into each other's eyes, his arm around her shoulders. Following them to the window, Poirot called after them, "Bless you, *mes enfants*! Oh, and if you encounter Miss Barbara in the garden, please ask her to return Captain Hastings to me. We must shortly begin our journey to London." Turning back into the room, his glance fell on the fireplace.

"Ah!" he exclaimed as he went to the mantelpiece over the fireplace and straightened the spill vase. "*Voilà!* Now, order and neatness are restored." With that, Poirot walked towards the door with an air of immense satisfaction.

AFTERWORD

It was almost certainly because of her dissatisfaction with someone else's stage adaptation of her Hercule Poirot novel, *The Murder of Roger Ackroyd,* in 1928, that my grandmother Agatha Christie decided to write a play of her own, which was something she had not previously attempted. *Black Coffee,* featuring her favourite detective, Poirot, was finished by the summer of 1929. But when Agatha showed it to her agent, he advised her not to bother submitting it to any theatrical management as, in his opinion, it was not good enough to be staged. Fortunately, a friend persuaded her to ignore such negative advice. The play was staged in 1930 at the Embassy Theatre, in Swiss Cottage, London.

Black Coffee was favourably received, and in April of the following year transferred to the West End of London, where it had a successful run of several months at the St. Martin's Theatre (where a later Christie play, *The Mousetrap,* began a much longer run in 1952). Poirot and his associate, Captain Hastings, were played by two popular actors of the time, Francis L. Sullivan and Roland Culver.

Some months later, *Black Coffee* was filmed in England at the Twickenham Studios, directed by Leslie Hiscott, with Austin Trevor as Poirot. The play remained a favourite with repertory companies for some years, and in 1956, Charles Osborne, then a young actor in England, found himself playing Dr. Carelli in *Black Coffee* in a summer season at Tunbridge Wells.

Nearly forty years later, after he had in the intervening years not only become a world authority on opera, but had also written a splendid book entitled *The Life and Crimes of Agatha Christie,* Osborne remembered the play. He suggested to Agatha Christie Ltd. (who control the copyright in her works) that, twenty years after the author's death, it would be marvellous to give the world a new Agatha Christie crime novel. We agreed enthusiastically, Osborne set to work, and the result is this Hercule Poirot murder mystery, which to me reads like authentic, vintage Christie. I feel sure Agatha would be proud to have written it.

—Mathew Prichard

BIOGRAPHICAL NOTE

Agatha Christie is the author of eighty crime novels and collections of stories, nineteen plays, and six novels written under the name of Mary Westmacott. Her books have sold over two billion copies worldwide in forty-four languages, and she is the most widely published author of all time in any language, outsold only by the Bible and Shakespeare.

Agatha Miller was born on September 15, 1890, in Torquay, Devonshire, England. She married Archie Christie, then a captain in the Royal Flying Corps, in 1914. In 1919, their daughter Rosalind was born.

Her first novel was written in response to a challenge from her sister, Madge, who did not believe she could write a good detective story. *The Mysterious Affair at Styles* was the result. In it, she created Hercule Poirot, the little Belgian detective with the egg-shaped head and the passion for order, not to mention the "little grey cells," who was destined to become the most popular detective in crime fiction since Conan Doyle's Sherlock Holmes. Published in the United States in 1920, it appeared in England the following year.

In 1926, she wrote what is still considered her masterpiece, *The Murder of Roger Ackroyd,* which became the first of Christie's books to be dramatized. Under the name *Alibi,* it had a successful run in the West End of London with Charles Laughton—in one of his first leading roles in the London theatre—playing the part of Poirot.

In 1930, Agatha Christie married for the second time, this time to archaeologist Max Mallowan, and began a life of great personal happiness. Nineteen-thirty also marked the publication of *Murder at the*

Vicarage, which introduced the deceptively mild Miss Marple.

Agatha Christie was awarded the CBE (Commander, Order of the British Empire) in 1956 and made a Dame Commander, Order of the British Empire, in 1971. In the mystery field, she was president of the Detection Club (1954) and awarded the Mystery Writers of America Grand-master Award (1955).

The Mousetrap, Christie's most famous play, was first produced as the radio play *Three Blind Mice,* commissioned by the BBC as a birthday treat for Queen Mary in 1947. Having run continuously since its West End debut in 1952, it is the longest running play in history.

Much of her work has been filmed for theatrical release as well as for television. Among the most famous films of her work are Rene Clair's *And Then There Were None,* Billy Wilder's *Witness for the Prosecution,* and Sidney Lumet's *Murder on the Orient Express.*

Agatha Christie died on January 12, 1976.